# BLACKSTONE RANGER CHIEF

### Blackstone Rangers Book 1

## ALICIA MONTGOMERY

Also by Alicia Montgomery

### THE TRUE MATES SERIES

Fated Mates

Blood Moon

Romancing the Alpha

Witch's Mate

Taming the Beast

Tempted by the Wolf

### THE LONE WOLF DEFENDERS SERIES

Killian's Secret

Loving Quinn

All for Connor

### THE TRUE MATES STANDALONE NOVELS

Holly Jolly Lycan Christmas

A Mate for Jackson: Bad Alpha Dads

### TRUE MATES GENERATIONS

A Twist of Fate

Claiming the Alpha

Alpha Ascending

A Witch in Time

Highland Wolf

Daughter of the Dragon

Shadow Wolf

A Touch of Magic

Heart of the Wolf

## THE BLACKSTONE MOUNTAIN SERIES

The Blackstone Dragon Heir

The Blackstone Bad Dragon

The Blackstone Bear

The Blackstone Wolf

The Blackstone Lion

The Blackstone She-Wolf

The Blackstone She-Bear

The Blackstone She-Dragon

## About the Author

Alicia Montgomery has always dreamed of becoming a romance novel writer. She started writing down her stories in now long-forgotten diaries and notebooks, never thinking that her dream would come true. After taking the well-worn path to a stable career, she is now plunging into the world of self-publishing.

 facebook.com/aliciamontgomeryauthor

twitter.com/amonromance

 bookbub.com/authors/alicia-montgomery

## Chapter 1

A bride walks into a bar.

No, it wasn't the start of a bad joke. It was actually *happening*.

Right now. On a Tuesday night in the middle of January.

And the moment she walked into The Den, she caught Damon Cooper's attention. But then again, who wouldn't stare? She sauntered right in like nobody's business, in a full-on, sparkly, frou-frou white concoction that trailed behind her.

*What the hell was going on?* And why, Damon wondered, couldn't he stop looking at her? He hadn't even seen her face, and now he itched to go over there so he could see the rest of her.

"I'm not seeing things, right?" Gabriel Russel asked, jaw dropped open.

"You mean, that hot, gorgeous little thing?" Anders Stevens piped in with a whistle. "Look at that body. I could get lost in—"

"Are you blind, man?" Daniel Rogers slapped him on the head. "She's wearing a wedding gown. Obviously, she's taken."

"Well, I don't see a groom anywhere," Anders said with a

shrug. "And what the hell is she doin' here, walking in dressed like that?"

Damon frowned. *What indeed.*

"Maybe she's lost?" Daniel offered.

"Or insane," Gabriel snorted. "I saw this made-for-TV movie once, where the woman's been abused by her fiancé. She snaps, kills the guy, and then puts on her wedding gown and drives off with his head on the front seat."

"So, what you're saying is, she's hot *and* crazy?" Anders raised a dark brow. "Sounds like a good combination."

"Really? *That's* what you gleaned from that story?" Gabriel looked at him incredulously.

"Hey, the craziest girls are the best in the sack," he said, unashamed.

"Oh, you mean like Darlene?" Gabriel shot back.

Anders winced. "Let's not talk about *that* mistake."

"I thought it was true love when she showed up at HQ, screaming and crying that she was going to kill herself if you didn't come out and talk to her," Daniel reminded him. "She's definitely one of the more memorable ones."

Anders took a swig of his drink and slammed it down. "Hey, I'm always up-front with women I fuck: One night, no strings. It's not my fault if they think they could be the one to 'tame' me." He snorted. "No one tames *this* tiger. Besides it's not like you two," he gestured to Gabriel and Daniel, "are innocent virgins knitting at home, waiting for your white knights."

"Hey, I can't help it if the ladies can't get enough of this gorgeous face and hair." Gabriel shook his thick head of golden hair in an exaggerated manner. The lion shifter really was handsome in the fairy-tale prince kind of way, and it was no wonder he had women fawning over him all the time.

"The only reason you haven't committed to anyone yet are those nosy sisters of yours, pretty boy," Daniel said.

"They're protective, that's all," Gabriel retorted. "I'm their only brother and the youngest, too."

"Speaking of the fabulous Russel sisters, do you think lionesses would go for a tiger?" Anders raised his brow.

Daniel nearly choked on his drink. "They'll eat you alive."

"And that's a bad thing?"

Gabriel's handsome face twisted in anger. "You stay away from my sisters, Stevens," he said with a quiet roar.

Damon was only half listening to their banter as his gaze was still fixed on the female. It was like the moment she entered the room; he couldn't turn away.

She was now seated on one of the barstools, waving an arm out to catch Tim Grimes's attention. The hulking polar bear was the owner of The Den, and on slow nights like this, he tended the bar. His back was turned to her, and when he finally did turn around, the look on the normally humorless bar owner was that of complete and utter shock.

The woman said something Damon couldn't make out. Even though he was a bear shifter and had heightened senses, they were still too far away. Tim looked at her, then pulled out a bottle of tequila from the shelf, filled up a shot glass before sliding it across the bar to her. With a nod of thanks, she knocked back the entire glass.

Anders rubbed his hands together. "Woohoo. Tequila is the mating call of desperate women. I think that's my signal, boys. I —Chief?"

Damon didn't even realize he had slammed his palm on Anders's chest to stop him from proceeding forward. *What the fuck?*

To his credit, Anders didn't say anything or take offense. He merely took a half step back.

"You okay, boss?" Daniel asked, a concerned look on his face.

As chief of the Blackstone Rangers—a position he'd only held for six months—he *was* technically their boss. But he'd worked with them for five years now, and he also considered them friends, Gabriel especially since they'd known each other since grade school.

"Yeah," he swallowed as his breathing became shallow. "I'm fine."

Gabriel's expression turned serious. "I know this is a lot for you, being out here." The lion shifter lowered his voice. "I wouldn't have suggested it except that you've been working your ass off for a week and deserve to relax. Plus, it's Tuesday, so I thought it wouldn't be packed. But with that blizzard keeping everyone cooped up last week, most people are rarin' to get out."

Right now, there were maybe a dozen people spread across the floor, but when he imagined it full of patrons, it was enough to make his chest tighten, and his bear started to get antsy. To say that crowds weren't their thing was a big understatement. The animal growled, and pain burst from behind his chest as its claws raked and its block head slammed against its human cage.

Back in high school, his tenaciousness on the football field had earned him the nickname The Demon, and he had carried it through his career in the Special Forces. But now it seemed the moniker was apt for different reasons. Reasons he'd rather forget.

He focused his attention on the woman. "I need a drink," he declared before stomping off toward the bar.

His eyes never left the woman in the wedding dress. Though her back was turned to him, he could see that she had long blonde hair tumbling down her bare shoulders and back. The crystal-studded torso clung to her curves, then fabric poofed out around her knees. As he drew nearer, his bear went eerily still. His gaze was fixed on the top of her head when she turned around.

Vivid blue eyes the color of pansies met his straight on, unblinking. Her face was ... perfection. A pert nose, high cheekbones, golden tanned skin, and lush lips that parted with a sharp breath. Locks and locks of shiny golden hair framed around her face.

But the thing that had made him and his bear stand up and take notice was the feeling that slammed into their chest.

*Mine.*

What. The. *Fuck.*

The Demon in him roared at the discovery. Honestly, Damon had thought that after that incident—*the* incident—landed him an honorable discharge from the army, his bear would be too broken and damaged to recognized its mate.

Or maybe it *was* and she wasn't their mate. After all, she was in a wedding gown so that meant she was taken, right?

The growl from The Demon rattled from his chest and was so loud, it made Tim snap his head toward him. "You all right there, Chief?" the polar bear shifter asked, a bushy white brow raised high.

"I-I'm fine. Whiskey, please," he said in a hoarse voice. "Double shot."

The woman—*his mate*—had turned away from him and was now hunched over her shot glass, which Tim had apparently refilled. Before he could even take a breath into his now rapidly-deflating lungs, she wrapped her fingers around the glass and drank the shot straight, pulling her head back dramatically so her blonde curls shook like waves of gold. Although she grimaced, she managed to slam the shot glass down and then waved her hand at Tim.

"Excuse me, bartender. Sir," she called out. "Can I have another, please?"

Her voice was soft and delicate, her tone posh and polite. Where did this woman come from? She certainly wasn't from

Blackstone. Except for his stint in the army, he'd lived here all his life, and he would have recognized her. Hell, he wouldn't have been able to forget her if their paths had crossed before.

As if sensing he was staring at her, her head turned, and her pansy-colored gaze narrowed at him. "Why don't you take a picture? It'll last longer," she snapped.

There was a spark of fire in her, and it only lit up his nerve endings—in a good way. His body was practically vibrating with need, and The Demon roared approvingly at their mate.

Clenching his teeth, he turned away and grabbed the glass Tim had set in front of him. He tossed a bill on the bar, not bothering to wait for his change.

*Fuck me.* He never thought he would meet his mate. Most shifters didn't have one, at least as far as he knew. His own parents, who were both Kodiak bear shifters like him, weren't mates, and they seemed content. No one really knew how you could find or meet your mate, but rather, you just knew. But that woman—that possibly *married* woman—was the other half of his soul?

*No thank you.*

The Demon did not like that one bit. It wanted him to go back and claim her, declare to the world who she was.

*Not happening,* he told his bear. They were not fit for a mate. Not since the incident. And certainly not after the fallout from it. He couldn't risk it. *Not again.*

Gabriel looked at him with concern. "You okay, man?"

Damon considered the lion shifter one of his best friends. He was the one who pulled him out from the darkness when he came home after being discharged. Kept him distracted after what happened and tried to make his life somewhat normal again. And, despite hating the outdoors, Gabriel even applied for the job with the rangers with him so he could keep him company throughout the training period, and even stuck around all these years when Gabriel didn't even need a job or the paycheck.

"Yeah." Damon took a swig of the whiskey. The burn did nothing to calm The Demon down, but the taste helped to ground him. Thankfully, it took a lot of liquor to get a shifter drunk, which was the only reason he didn't turn into a raging alcoholic or drug addict after leaving the Special Forces.

"So, is she even hotter up close?" Anders said.

A growl got stuck in his throat as Damon managed to control his bear. "Didn't notice." The animal chuffed. *Lie. Total lie,* it seemed to say as it shook its fur. Their mate was gorgeous. The most beautiful female in the world.

"Better make your move, Anders," Daniel said. "Looks like we're not the only ones who noticed her."

Damon whipped his head back to the bar. Two men had approached her and stood on either side, trying to engage her in conversation. But she didn't acknowledge them and instead waved to Tim to refill her shot glass again.

*Good.*

Though she continued to ignore them and hunched further around her shot glass, the males didn't seem to pay her disinterest any mind. They continued their efforts to gain her attention, their voices getting louder even as she pretended not to hear them and took another shot of tequila.

The glass in his hand cracked audibly as his fist tightened around it.

"Jesus, Damon, what the fuck?" Anders exclaimed as bits of broken glass exploded around them.

His entire body froze as one of the men drew closer, his arm going around her shoulders, which she shrugged right off. The snarl that escaped his throat was inhuman, and before he knew it, he was stalking back to the bar.

"... please get your hands off me," she said in a polite tone even as she shrugged the man's arm away again.

"Aww, darlin', don't be like that," the man slurred. "I just wanna get to know—"

"The lady doesn't want your company," Damon growled.

The man's spine stiffened, then he turned around. "Why don't you mind your bus—Jesus Christ!"

Sweat and panic rolled off the man as Damon opened his mouth to bare his growing fangs. *Human*, Damon's shifter senses told him. Probably a tourist wanting to have a look-see at the shifters living in Blackstone. The Den was a known shifter hangout, after all.

*We can't hurt him.* They'd shred the man into ribbons without breaking a sweat.

But The Demon couldn't be reasoned with, not in this state, not when it was seeing red. It wanted to rip the man's arms off for touching what was theirs. Another inhuman growl rattled from his chest, and he knew that the muscles underneath his skin were moving as The Demon fought for control.

"Fuck!" The man yelped as a hand that was human, but now sprouting fur, wrapped around his neck. Black claws were extending from the tip, scraping against the man's delicate skin.

"Damon, calm the fuck down."

It sounded like Gabriel, but the blood roaring in Damon's ears was too loud. The Demon was ready to kill.

A gigantic paw covered in white fur slammed down on the bar so hard, the various shot glasses and mugs clattered across the surface. "Can it, Chief," Tim ordered. The older man was not someone to be messed with, both in human and polar bear form. "This is *my* bar, and you know the rules. No shifting."

Despite the fear Damon could still taste in the air, the man smiled smugly at him. "You heard him. Let go of me."

He bared his teeth one last time at the offending human,

then loosened his grip and dropped his hands to his sides.

"I see you know your place." The man spat on the ground. "Filthy animal."

There was a loud roar, and though Damon thought it had come from him, he was wrong. It was Tim who let out the teeth-rattling, bone shaking growl.

"Oh shit!" Someone—Daniel, it sounded like—exclaimed before all hell broke loose.

Tim slammed both paws on the bar and then hopped over in one leap. For a huge man, who also turned into the largest bear in the world, he moved quickly, and soon he was advancing toward the two humans as his bones cracked and fur began to sprout all over his body.

"Fuck!" They couldn't let Tim harm those humans. The anti-shifter organizations would be all over the place with their damn protests. "Guys—"

"We're on it, Chief." Anders cracked his neck and rolled his shoulders, then charged toward Tim. The tiger shifter could be lethal even without shifting into his animal form.

Damon's next concern, of course, was the woman. He had to get her out—

"What the hell?"

She was gone.

The Demon roared in urgency, and pushed him forward and out the door. He didn't sniff her scent, so he couldn't track her with his nose, but there was only one exit here.

It didn't take him too long to find her; she was like a beacon in that gown as she walked out of the parking lot toward the darkened road. There was an oncoming truck that she didn't see as she continued to lumber forward.

With his superhuman speed, he caught up to her just as she was about to step into the truck's path, then grabbed her arm. Unfortunately, he forgot his own strength as he pulled her, sending them both to the ground. His back slammed into concrete as puffs of tulle and a soft body landed on top of him.

"Hey!"

Arms grappled his as she pushed herself off him. As she struggled to get up, he groaned as her knees hit his abdomen. *At least she didn't aim lower.*

Her weight lifted off him as she scrambled to the side. He got to his feet and let out another groan as he felt a different pain from his nether regions. She was on all fours and her gown had pushed her cleavage up, breasts nearly bursting from the top of her neckline. Fuck, his zipper was practically imprinting on his dick.

Brushing herself off, she got up. "Whaddidya you do that for?" she slurred. "I ... it's you."

The tequila was strong on her breath, and she swayed on her feet. "Are you okay, miss?"

"Me? I'm fiiiine ..." She hiccupped. "I just ... I don't usually drink that much." Her eyes were unfocused. "Are you ..."

Her body fell forward, and he easily caught her. His arms slipped around her waist and pulled her against his chest. As her sweet scent wrapped around him, he cursed inwardly. The Demon, on the other hand, yowled with delight.

*Yowl with delight?* That damned bear didn't like anything or anyone. It hated almost everything in the world.

"You have pretty eyes." She was looking straight up at him. "They're so green." Her hand reached up to cup his jaw, and his spine—and other parts of him—went stiff.

"Uh ... miss, can I take you home? Or to your hotel? Should I call your husband?" That last part left a bitter taste in his mouth.

"I'm not ... no husband." She frowned, and her hands dropped to her sides. "I ran away. Jilted him at the altar, as they say."

Relief poured through him. So, she wasn't married. Of course, that didn't mean she was *free*. "Where do you live, miss? Maybe I can call your family or something."

"Nowhere. Not anymore," she bawled, tears springing to her eyes. "I can't go back now. Not after what I've done."

Goddamn, he hated waterworks, but seeing her cry made him want to rip something apart. But he didn't know how to comfort her. "How about a friend, maybe you can stay with a friend? Do you know someone in town? How did you get here?"

"I drove," she stated.

"From?"

"From the church."

"Which church?" He scrambled for names of nearby churches. "Saint Joseph's in Greenville? Or the one in Verona Mills?"

"All Saints Episcopalian," she said.

"I've never heard of that one. Is that the one on seventy-five?"

"It's back home."

"And where is home?"

She smiled dreamily. "Why, in Albuquerque, silly."

"Albu—as in *New Mexico*?" he asked incredulously.

"Is there another Albuquerque?"

*Christ.* That was about an eight-hour drive from here. How in the world did she get all the way to Blackstone? And what was he going to do now? "I can't leave you out here, miss. Is there somewhere I can take you to? A motel? Or the hospital?"

"You can take me home."

The Demon thought that was a very good idea, but he pushed those thoughts away. "I don't think—" He stopped as her head rolled back and her eyes closed. Then she started snoring softly, and her body turned into a dead weight in his arms.

*Goddammit.*

# Chapter 2

*What in all things good and holy happened last night?*

Based on the pounding headache drilling into her brain, Anna Victoria Hall knew that whatever it was, it *wasn't* good.

And it probably involved tequila.

*Good Lord.* Any time she had the stuff, bad things happened. Like now, for example, waking up in a strange place. In a strange *bed*.

"No, no, no." The world spun as she sat up like a rocket. "Ooof." Normally, this was about the time she told herself, *I'm never drinking again.* And maybe this time she really meant it.

*I've really done it now.*

Slowly, she opened her eyes. She was in some kind of ... log cabin? It smelled like pine in here and something ... very masculine. The dark furniture, the flannel sheets, and the distinct maleness in her surroundings told her this was definitely a man's bedroom.

"What have you gotten yourself into, Anna Victoria Hall?" she whispered to herself.

This wasn't how she wanted her day to end up. Hell's bells,

this wasn't how she thought her life would end up—hungover on tequila, in a stranger's bedroom, on the day after what was supposed to be her wedding.

The memories suddenly slammed into her befuddled brain and the pain in her head pounded even harder.

*Maybe I should have gone through with it.*

But the thought had barely formed in her head before her skin started crawling. Marrying Edward Jameson would have been a mistake. But it's not like she had a choice in the first place.

She took a deep breath and frowned. *Why was it hard to breathe?* Glancing down, she realized she was still wearing the most hideous wedding gown ever created. *I wouldn't have chosen something so tacky, even if I wanted to get married.* No, this crime against fashion had been the groom's choice, along with other aspects of that farce of a wedding.

The moment she'd laid eyes on the gown, she'd hated it—not just because it was gaudy, but because of what it represented. But she'd never been happier to be wearing it than she was at this moment. The damned thing took two seamstresses to put on, and so that meant she'd kept it on all night. That meant she didn't just have sex with some stranger on what was supposed to be her wedding night.

But the question still remained: *Where the hell was she?*

Burying her face in her hands, she dug into her brain for the last of her memories. Waiting in the back of the church. Realizing this was a mistake. And then sneaking out the front door and taking a taxi back to her apartment. There had been no time to do anything—not to pack, not to get dressed, and certainly not to plan. She took out the daily maximum of cash from her debit card during a quick stop at the drive-through ATM, then took off. Somewhere along the highway, she dumped her phone, debit and credit cards—even if her father hadn't cut them off yet, it was too risky to use them.

Of course, she wasn't *completely* destitute. In fact, sitting in the trunk of her car was a duffel bag full of cash. But she would starve and die before she touched *that* money.

"Oh Lord."

More memories flooded back. The bar last night. And tequila. A lot of it. Too much. And then ... she remembered big, strong arms around her. A masculine scent that seemed imprinted in her brain.

A throat clearing made her freeze. "You're up."

The rough, sleep-hewn quality of the voice made her shiver. In a good way. Slowly, she turned her head toward the source.

*Oh no.*

Despite the fact that her brain couldn't piece together what happened after the fourth or fifth shot of tequila, what it did remember was *this* guy. And she recognized him immediately. How could she not, when he had stared at her so openly when he approached the bar? Not even her tequila-dulled senses could ignore the spark of desire in his bright green eyes—or the one in her core—which was why she had been vastly disappointed when he just turned and walked away after he got his drink. The rejection spurned her on to take more shots of tequila.

From where he stood in the doorway, he didn't move, didn't say anything. The man just kept staring at her. Oh God, he was even cuter than she remembered. Handsome actually. Strong, chiseled jaw with a little dent in the chin. She remembered it being clean-shaven last night, but this morning, there was a bit of scruff on it. His shoulders were broad and looked like they were built like rocks, the muscles underneath the golden bronzed skin stretching out his white T-shirt while various

15

tattoos dotted down his brawny arms. He was tall, too, probably a couple of inches over six feet.

Her mouth went dry, like she'd coughed up sand. Glancing to her left, she saw a glass of water and two tablets. Ignoring the unmarked medicine—because she was hungover, not stupid—she grabbed the glass and chugged down as much as she could without choking.

"Better?"

God, it was like his voice plucked this string inside her that made her body vibrate. "Y-y-es. Thank you." An awkward silence stretched between them. "Um, I was wondering, could you tell me ... where we are?"

"In my house."

Right, she guessed that much. "But what am I doing here?"

"You asked me to take you home."

Embarrassment coursed through her, all the way to the tips of her toes. "I-I did?"

He nodded.

"I'm sure I didn't mean it. I mean, not to your home." Oh God, had they ... done anything? For some reason, that didn't make her feel embarrassed—only disappointed that she hadn't remembered anything at all.

"You walked out of The Den, and I saw you were about to cross the street. Nearly stepped in front of a truck." He took a few steps toward the bed. "And then you said you drove here from New Mexico."

"And here is ...?"

"Blackstone. Colorado." His brows wrinkled. "You don't know where you are?"

She shook her head. "I was just passing through. I needed to rest since I'd been driving nearly non-stop from New Mexico, and I had a cramp in my leg, and so I stopped at that bar. I didn't mean to start drinking, but I figured I deserved just one, and if I ate a huge dinner it would be fine, but it felt so warm and—" Oh God, she was babbling. "So, this town is called Blackstone?"

"Technically we're in the Blackstone Mountains, outside of the town."

"And what are we doing in the Blackstone Mountains?"

"You asked me to take you—"

"Yeah, I got that part." Her head was throbbing again.

"There's medicine for you next to the water. Should help with the headache."

She didn't make a move and instead picked at some non-existent lint on the sheet. "I'm so sorry. For the inconvenience." The man remained silent, but moved closer. "I—" When she looked up, startlingly clear green eyes were staring at her, and her stomach flipped. "Did we ..." Her hands gestured nervously at the bed.

"No." His jaw hardened. "You passed out in my arms, and I brought you here. I slept downstairs on the couch."

Although she'd already guessed that nothing happened because she would have needed a damn can opener to get her out of this dress, somehow, his confirmation disappointed her. *Stop being silly, Anna Victoria Hall.* Not having drunken sex with a stranger was a *good thing.*

"Again, I'm sorry." Shimmying to the edge of the bed, she slung her legs over the side. "I just—whoa!"

The world spun again and another dizzy spell came over her, sending her toward the floor. She braced herself for the impact, but it never came. Instead, two strong arms caught her and pulled her up against a hard chest. That faint masculine scent that she had smelled on the sheets surrounded her now, so delicious and tempting that she had to take a whiff.

"Uh, miss?"

Unfortunately, to take that whiff, she had to press her nose against the very hard, very male chest she had been propped against. Quickly, she pulled her face away from him.

*If any god is up there or downstairs, please strike me dead now.*

He remained silent, but his hand went up to her cheek. His touch was soft and gentle, and despite the clenching of his jaw, there was a surprising tenderness in his eyes. Her heart thudded against her chest at the gentleness of his touch.

"You have some, uh, stuff there." His fingers brushed at her skin, rubbing away some sleep crust from the corner of her eye.

Her cheeks aflame, she stood up and pushed off him. "Uh, thanks." How did he get to her so fast? "I need to use the bathroom."

He cocked his head at the door on the right. "Over there."

Brushing past him, she quickly dashed to the door. As soon as it closed, she let out a sigh, then looked up at the mirror.

"Oh, poop." Her skin was sallow, and the bags under her eyes had bags. It was a good thing during one of her pit stops, she managed to find some makeup wipes at a gas station convenience store, otherwise, she'd surely be sporting mascara raccoon eyes.

After washing her face and doing her business, she looked down at the dress with a deep sigh. *How am I going to get out of this thing?* Even if she did manage to get this bedazzled monstrosity off her, she didn't exactly have anything else to wear.

A knock on the door knocked her out of her thoughts. "Yes?"

"I have some clothes for you, in case you wanted to change. When you're done, you can come downstairs."

"Oh." *That was nice of him.* "Thank you. I'll be right out." Okay, now the only thing she had to figure out was how to free herself from this testament of bad taste. *Maybe there's something I could use around here.*

The bathroom was sparse, but spotless and clean. A hand towel hung from a hook to the right of the mirror, while a bar of soap sat on a dish beside the faucet. She reached for the drawers, only hesitating because she didn't want to invade his privacy since that's where most people kept their personal items. When she pulled one open, she was surprised to see that inside was neat and everything in its place—extra toothbrushes lined up in a row, a package of floss in the corner, new razors beside it. There had to be something here ... there! A pair of scissors glinted when she pulled the drawer out further.

With a deep sigh, she positioned the scissors in the middle of the sweetheart neckline. *How ironic.* Her teeth ground together as she sliced down the middle, and suddenly, she could breathe again. She was finally free. Literally and figuratively.

Shrugging the rest of the gown off, she grabbed the hand towel and gave herself a quick sponge bath, then rinsed her mouth out multiple times with water from the tap. That deep tub in the corner looked tempting, but she was pretty sure the man who owned this house would mind very much if she took a bubble bath.

Her fingers massaged the bridge of her nose. *I don't even know his name.*

Marching out of the bathroom with the remains of the dress, she spotted a large paper bag, and inside were the clothes he mentioned. They consisted of a pair of leggings, a heavy sweater, and thick socks. As she put them on, it dawned on her where these clothes could have come from. *Oh God, he has a girlfriend. Or a wife.*

Somehow, the thought of that made her chest seize up; why, she didn't know. However, looking around, there were no signs of a feminine hand anywhere. Much like the bathroom, the bedroom was utilitarian—the only furniture was the bed, side table, and a dresser. There were no knickknacks anywhere, no clothes piled in the corner or surfaces, and everything was clean as a whistle. Maybe these clothes were left by an ex. Or a one-night stand. None of those thoughts comforted her, so she pushed them aside.

Now somewhat presentable, she could go downstairs, but there was the matter of the dress. It would be rude to just leave it here for him to discard, so she balled it up as tightly as possible and shoved it into the empty bag.

*He had said to come downstairs.* Now, she wasn't dumb; he was a stranger and she was in his house, so the smart thing to do would be to sneak out while she could. However, the rational part of her said that if he wanted to harm her, he'd have done it by now or while she was sleeping. Perhaps there were still some really good Samaritans in the world.

In any case, maybe he could give her a ride back to her car. That damned dress didn't have any pockets, so she left her purse inside and only took some cash and her keys. Hopefully she'd dropped her keys in the bar, but if not, maybe she could call a locksmith, at least to get her purse and figure out what to do next.

Padding out of the room, she headed toward the stairs, paper bag in her hand. The smell of coffee, toast, and bacon filled her nostrils. Her stomach gurgled embarrassingly, but grease and caffeine were exactly what her hungover-self needed right now.

As she descended the stairs, she walked past the living room and into the kitchen. Her eyes immediately went to the tall, dark-haired man hunched over the stove, and her stomach did that flippy thing again. *Oh jeez, the back view was just as spectacular as the front.*

"Good morning, sunshine."

The voice made her start. To her surprise, there was another man sitting at the breakfast nook, someone she'd never seen before.

In all her twenty-five years on this earth, she'd been around a lot of good-looking men before but this guy ... he wasn't just handsome, he was actually *beautiful*. His features were refined, almost angelic. And, as if to emphasize that point, the dark golden mane of hair around him lit up like a halo. Blue eyes twinkled with amusement when their gazes met.

"Uh, good morning," she managed to say.

"I have to say, I was so surprised when Damon asked me to come here and bring some clothes that I just had to stay and find out for whom." His perfect, bow-shaped mouth quirked up into a smile. "I wondered where he went when he disappeared last night. Never thought I'd see that day. Why, he's practically a monk—"

"Gabriel." The man—Damon, apparently—had turned around, a fierce scowl marring his face. "Didn't I tell you to leave?"

"You mean, after I drove all the way out here to do you a favor?" He quirked a golden brow at her. "But I can see why you'd want me out as soon as possible." Hopping off the stool, he stalked toward her, his movements lithe and graceful. He was tall, like Damon, though built differently. Whereas the dark-haired man was built like a linebacker, this man had the body of a dancer—long limbed and lean, though with a power underneath that shouldn't be underestimated. "Gabriel Russel, at your service." He held out his hand, but when Damon let out a strange rumbling sound, he quickly retracted it.

"Anna Victoria Hall." She gestured to the clothes. "Uh, these yours?"

"Nah, they're my sister Ginny's." He tapped a finger on his chin. "Or maybe Giselle's. Could also be Gwen's."

How many sisters did this man have? "I'm sorry to have

troubled her. And you." The idea that the clothing wasn't a wife or girlfriend or one-night stand's made her sigh in relief.

"No trouble at all. My sisters leave their shit around my apartment all the time."

"Eat." Damon had placed a plate and a mug of coffee on the breakfast nook, on the end farthest away from Gabriel. "It'll help with the hangover. You were pretty drunk last night, so I imagine it's a killer."

Her cheeks warmed at the reminder. Oh God, what else did she do last night? The humiliation nearly made her turn tail and run out the door. But the bacon smelled too good, so she sat herself on the stool and took a bite, the greasy, crispy strip breaking into pieces as it melted inside her mouth. "Hmm," she moaned and closed her eyes. It was perfectly cooked. "Oohhh," she said, licking her lips.

Gabriel let out a chuckle, which made her snap out of her near-orgasmic state. The hairs on the back of her neck prickled as she realized Damon was staring at her again, and those clear green eyes were fixed on her lips. A sizzle of heat went up her spine, but he turned his back to her before she could react any further.

"So, Anna Victoria," Gabriel began. "Tell me more about yourself. How did you meet Damon?"

"I ... uh, don't remember," she confessed. "I had too much tequila last night and then ... I woke up in his bed." Oh God, the way that sounded. "I didn't ... I mean we didn't ..." Did someone come in here and set her cheeks on fire? Because it sure felt like they did. She took a sip from the mug. "Maybe I should start again."

Gabriel glanced down at the paper bag by her feet, then looked at her. "Oh. My. God. It was you."

*You?* How did this man know who she was?

His jaw dropped, then he slowly turned to Damon. "You have some explaining to do."

"It's not what you think," Damon said in a gruff tone as he began to clean up the stove. "I didn't exactly have a choice."

His dismissive tone stung much harder than it should have. "I can explain." At least she thought she could. The small burst of caffeine was working into her system, so she could piece together the events of last night. "I had too much tequila at the bar, and I walked outside to get some air. Then I passed out. Mr., er, Damon found me and brought me here because, as he said, he didn't have a choice." His back stiffened. "I'm sorry. For all the trouble." She swallowed the lump in her throat. "I'll get out of your way now." She slid off the stool and walked out of the kitchen, making her way to the door.

Why did he act so cold all of a sudden? When she woke up this morning, he'd been anything but. She even thought he was so sweet, getting those clothes for her and making her breakfast. Then there was the unmistakable heat in his eyes she couldn't get out of her mind.

Now he acted like she was a complete inconvenience, which in retrospect, she *was*. Had she read him wrong? But still, he didn't have to make her feel so ... unwanted. The thought bristled at her, and for the umpteenth time that morning, she asked herself why the opinion of a stranger should matter to her.

Yanking the door open, she stepped outside onto the porch. "Holy—"

Everything outside was covered in snow. Though they got snow in Albuquerque, it was never like this. The scene was almost magical—if she wasn't so cold. The thick socks weren't enough to keep the chill out, and her body gave an involuntary shiver.

*Now what am I going to do?* She had no car, no money, and

nowhere to go. Maybe running out at her wedding was a mistake.

No, marrying Edward Jameson would have been the biggest mistake of her life.

"Anna Victoria?"

She whirled around, and couldn't help but feel disappointed when she realized it was Gabriel who had chased after her. "Hey," she said. "Um, I'll be out of your way, as soon as I figure out how to get to my car. How far is it to walk to that bar?"

"What? Are you crazy?" he said. "Way too far. You'll never make it. The ground's still frozen, thanks to this crazy blizzard we had over the weekend."

"Oh." Her lip trembled and her throat tightened. "I guess I could call a cab." There was still money in the purse. And then there was the duffel bag stashed in the trunk. "Hold onto this, for me, okay, darling?" her 'fiancé' had asked. "I'll take it back after the honeymoon. It's just some old junk I need moved out of the penthouse."

*Old junk, my behind.* But thinking about where the money came from made her shiver again—and it wasn't because of the cold.

"You're not going anywhere," Gabriel said, knocking her out of her thoughts.

His words made her double-blink. "I-I'm not?"

"I mean, not without me."

"Excuse me?"

"I'll take you into town," he said. "To your car."

"Oh. Wow. Thank you so much, Gabriel." Normally, she would have protested, but what choice did she have? It was better than being stuck here with that man scowling at her and making her feel so unwelcome.

"Don't thank me. Damon pretty much ordered me to do it,"

he said with a chuckle. "He's my boss and all, but also my best friend, so we're good."

Boss? She wanted to ask what they did, but bit her lip. It wasn't like she was going to be around long enough for it to matter.

"Are you ready?" he asked. "I got this for you too." A paper bag dangled from his fingers.

She grimaced at the sight of the tulle peeking from the top and grabbed the bag. "I wouldn't want to leave it behind for him to clean up."

"I also have a pair of boots for you, but I left them in my truck." he cocked his head at the shiny red Jeep in the driveway, "if you don't mind being barefoot for a couple more feet, we can get out of here."

Pausing, she glanced back at the front door, as if she was waiting for something ... for him to come after her? She snorted. Highly unlikely. Damon looked like he couldn't wait to get her out of there. "Lead the way," she said.

———

Not that she thought Gabriel was lying, but she definitely would not have made it all the way back to the bar—The Den, as he called it—on foot. Damon lived in the middle of nowhere, deep in the mountains, and it took them nearly an hour to drive all the way into town. Blackstone looked like any small mountain town, with a bustling little Main Street with mom-and-pop shops, cafes, and restaurants, though she did see signs of development, such as modern condos, recreational areas, and shopping and entertainment complexes.

Gabriel continued to drive them out of the main town area, and soon they were pulling into a parking lot off the main road.

"Over there," she said, pointing to the lone car in the middle of the lot.

He whistled. "Nice ride."

Her silver Mercedes was about a year old, a Christmas present from her father. "I think I lost the keys in the bar," she said sadly. But at least it was still here, and it appeared intact. "If you want to leave me here, I can wait until the bar opens up and check inside."

"The Den won't be open until at least lunchtime, and that's still a couple of hours away," he said.

"I don't mind."

"Damon'll kill me if I left you alone," he grumbled.

"Huh?" She cocked her head to the side. "Why would he care what happens to me? He seemed like he couldn't wait to get rid of me."

Placing his hands on the wheel, he let out a sigh. "Don't let him get to you. Damon's just ... well ... it's hard to explain."

"No need," she huffed. "It doesn't matter. I'll be outta here soon. That is, once I get my keys. I think I have some gym clothes in the trunk, so I can give these clothes back to you. Or I can mail them back."

"Keep 'em. My sisters have tons of clothes. But still, I can't leave you alone out here. Even if it is my day off."

Now she really felt bad. "I'm so sorry, Gabriel. Really, you don't have to—"

"Say, how about we go get some brunch? I know a place that serves up some good pies." He turned that megawatt smile on her. "I mean, at least you can pass the time somewhere warm with great food and coffee."

"I—why would you do that?" she said. "You hardly know me."

There was an unreadable expression on his face. "Let's just say, I have a feeling about you."

"A feeling? What kind of feeling?"

"I'll tell you another time," he said.

"Another time? I won't be staying here long enough."

He shrugged. "Anyway, how about it?"

"Well ..." She didn't get a chance to finish the breakfast Damon had made for her. "If you don't mind."

"I was going to meet a friend for brunch anyway. And I'm already running late."

"Oh. I wouldn't want to intrude—"

"Nah, don't worry. J.D. won't mind, you'll see."

"I guess that's okay. My purse is in my car though, so you'll have to pay first. I promise I'll pay you right back."

"Sure." He put the car into gear. "You'll love Rosie's. She has the best pies in the world."

Gabriel turned the Jeep around, and soon they were back on Main Street. He pulled up into an empty spot in front of an establishment that proclaimed "Rosie's Bakery and Cafe" on the sign above the door. After parking the car, he slid out the door, and she followed suit, letting herself out of the Jeep's passenger side. He opened the door and motioned for her to go inside first.

The smell of buttery pastries and fresh coffee hit her nose, making her stomach grumble. "It smells divine in here." The interior decor was all pink and cheery, and at the far end was a large display case full of pies. "Oh my God. They make all those here?"

"From scratch," Gabriel proclaimed proudly. "This place is the best." He scanned the dining room before his face lit up in recognition. "Looks like J.D.'s already here."

They crossed the room, with her following behind him until they reached a booth on the other side. There was someone already sitting at the booth, whose face was obscured by a trucker hat. "Jesus, Russel, we all know it takes, like, five hours to get your hair done, but you could have called that you're running late. I'm starving."

Anna Victoria double blinked, surprised at the feminine voice. The person waiting for Gabriel was a woman, apparently. A pretty, delicate face peeked out from the under the hat's brim, and hazel eyes framed by thick blonde lashes flickered with annoyance.

"Really?" she groused. "You kept me waiting because of a *girl*?"

Anna Victoria swallowed. "I'm sorry," she glanced worryingly at Gabriel. "I didn't mean to—"

"Shush, sweetheart." He put a hand up. "Why you ridin' my ass hard this morning, J.D.? You on the rag or something?"

"Fuck you, pretty boy," she scowled. "You're late, so you're paying."

Gabriel grinned. "Fine, but you won't believe what I got to tell you, and who this is," he nodded to Anna Victoria.

J.D. rolled her eyes. "Tell me something I haven't heard before."

"This is *her*," Gabriel said. "The one I told you about last night. The girl at The Den who got Damon all riled up."

Hazel eyes went wide as J.D. stared up at her. "The chick in the wedding gown?"

Anna Victoria felt heat creep up neck. That's what Gabriel meant when he said *it was you*, this morning. "You were there last night?"

"Yeah. I saw you walk into The Den, plant yourself on that barstool, and start knocking back tequila like a fucking champ," he chuckled, then turned to J.D. "I thought I was seeing things. Little did I know she and Damon had gotten busy—"

"We didn't. Nothing happened. I just passed out, and he helped me." Humiliation flooded her veins. "I'm not like that ... I mean, that's not ... something I do regularly."

"Huh." His eyes narrowed. "I wonder why he was so—hey, what's wrong?"

Her bottom lip trembled. They must both think she was some kind of ... hussy. After all, she was in a wedding gown, then wound up in another man's bed. "This was a mistake. I should go—" She attempted to turn around but a hand on her arm stopped her. "Gab—" But to her surprise, it was J.D.'s hand on her.

The other woman's expression was that of sympathy. "Hey, don't mind this idiot here," J.D. began. "He may think he's smooth with the ladies, but his sisters have spoiled him so rotten he doesn't know when he's acting like a dumbass." She glared at Gabriel before asking, "So, what's your name?"

"Anna Victoria."

"Well, Anna Victoria, I'm J.D. Obviously, you've been through—or are going through—a lot, and I'm sorry for that. But why don't you stay and have a bite to eat?"

"I'm intruding on your date."

"Date?" J.D. laughed. "If this is a date, then I'm the fucking prom queen. C'mon, girl. You don't have to talk or bare your soul, but you do gotta eat, right? Gabriel will make up for being an asshat by paying for both our meals. God knows he can afford it."

Well, she was still hungry, and those pies in the display case looked amazing. "All right." She slid in beside J.D., and Gabriel took the seat opposite them.

"So," Gabriel began. "Why were you in a wedding dress when you walked in The Den—ow! Dammit J.D.!"

The other woman had taken her trucker cap off, reached over, and smacked Gabriel on the head with it. With a smug smile, J.D. tucked her messy blonde ponytail under the cap and turned to Anna Victoria. "I mean it, you don't have to tell us anything if you don't want to."

"T-thank you." And she really didn't want to. J.D. and Gabriel seemed like nice people, and she didn't want to involve them in her personal affairs.

"I do want all the details about last night." She pointed her finger at Gabriel. "You said you'd make it worth my time."

Gabriel glanced nervously at Anna Victoria. "Why don't we order first?" He waved to a passing waitress who was holding a pot of coffee. "Rosie, my love," he said. "You're looking even more beautiful every day."

The woman stopped and turned, her lips curling up into a grin. "My, my, Gabriel Russel. To what do I owe this honor?"

Anna Victoria tried to guess the woman's age, but it was difficult. Though there were some lines around the corners of her mouth and eyes, her skin was still smooth, her hair was a vibrant red, and her vintage-style dress with polka-dots hugged her trim figure. Her piercing green eyes, though, made her seem like an old soul.

"The honor is mine." He bowed his head. "And you do have the best pies in town."

Rosie patted him on the shoulder and laughed. "What can I get you? The usual for you, Gab? A slice of cherry, a slice of pecan, and a slice of lemon merengue all with extra whipped cream?"

He flashed her that million-dollar smile. "You know me so well."

"Yeah, well you never order anything else, even when you were this"—she held her hand about waist high—"tall. And, ladies? What can I get ya?"

"Just apple for me this morning, Rosie," J.D. said.

Rosie's green eyes narrowed at Anna Victoria. "I've never seen you here before. Are you new in town?"

She bristled. "I'm just passing through."

"I don't mean to be rude, honey." Rosie smiled at her. "I've known most of the patrons here since they were kids, and now they bring *their* kids here. So, I usually already know what people want."

"Oh." She didn't mean to snap at the older lady, but it had been a trying twenty-four hours. "Well, what would you recommend?"

"We have the classics; apple, pecan, key lime, pumpkin, chocolate, etcetera. But," she tapped a finger on her chin. "I've got a new employee in training who's been experimenting with some new flavors. How does chai latte cream pie sound?"

Gabriel grimaced. "Chai latte cream pie? What the fuck is that?"

"Actually, that sounds amazing," she said. "I'll have one please."

"Give me a slice, too, will ya, Rosie?" J.D. added.

"Ugh." Gabriel made a face. "Rosie, my love, please don't tell me you're turning this place into some kind of hipster hang out."

Rosie chuckled. "No way, kiddo. But, sometimes we gotta innovate, you know, to keep up? Blackstone is booming with all these new cafes and businesses, so I need to stay competitive."

"I'll eat my weight in pie everyday if that'll help," Gabriel offered. "Just please don't change a thing."

"Thanks, hon. You've always been my favorite."

"I bet ya say that to all the guys," he retorted playfully.

"But with you, it's the truth." She patted him on the cheek. "All right. I'll get those orders in for you and two more cups of joe." Her skirt twirled as she turned on her heel and walked toward the counter of pies.

"Now," J.D. said as she hunched forward and cupped the mug of coffee in her hands. "Last night. Spill."

Anna Victoria wasn't sure she wanted to hear this, but then

again, it might solve a few burning questions in her mind, like, how the heck she ended up in Damon's bed.

"So, all of us—Anders, Daniel, and me—finally get one night off together, so we decide to head to The Den, of course. And Damon, well you know him—because of that freak blizzard last week we've all been pullin' doubles—"

"Which means he's been there the entire time," J.D. finished with a cluck of her tongue.

"Yeah. Didn't sleep for three days straight until we found every single person caught out in the storm. Anyway, he's been wound up tight, so we guilt him into coming with us, since it's a Tuesday and all. We're there having a couple of drinks when Anna Victoria walks in."

She tensed as the memory came back to her. Why, oh why did she even choose to go into that bar?

"Anyway, Anders is doing his usual shtick, but it's Damon who goes to her." He flashed her a grin. "We thought he was going to hit on you or something, which he never does, by the way. Hit on girls, I mean. Not that he isn't interested in girls! He is, but ... er, anyway, it turns out he just wanted a drink."

The disappointment she had felt when he turned away came back to her like a sharp knife slicing against her skin. Again, why did she feel that way toward a man she hardly knew?

"Then," Gabriel continued, "a while later, these two human assholes start sniffing around her, and Damon goes apeshit on their asses."

Her jaw nearly dropped to the floor. "He did?"

J.D. looked at her incredulously. "How much did you drink?"

"Too much. Tequila has that effect on me," she groaned. "Most of it was a blur. Those guys were trying to talk to me, but I was ignoring them. I think ... I remember while they were distracted, I really had to go to the bathroom, but I must have gotten lost and gone outside instead."

"Humans," he snorted. "Anyway, Tim comes down on him and everything's seemingly fine. That's when those two bastards call Damon a ..." His voice lowered. "A filthy animal."

J.D.'s lips peeled back and her teeth bared. "Motherfucker."

"Yeah. Tim went *nuts*. So Anders, Daniel and I get ready to pull him back, but Damon just disappears just as Tim finishes shifting into his polar bear—"

"Wait—*what?*" Anna Victoria blinked, not sure she heard him right.

Two pairs of eyes stare back at her. "Shifted. Into his polar bear," Gabriel said matter-of-factly before his jaw slackened. "You don't know?"

"That the bartender is a ... a ..."

"A shifter," J.D. finished, her mouth pursing together. "Do you have a problem with that?"

"No!" she said quickly. Everyone knew about shifters of course, and back in Albuquerque, they had been around, though there weren't many. According to what she'd read, most of them didn't like city life and lived in more remote areas. "I mean, I'm not one of those people who say, 'I can't be prejudiced, I have shifter friends,' because there aren't a lot back home. But I'm more of a live and let live kind of person, you know?"

"But then, why did come here?" J.D. asked.

"To Blackstone? I didn't really have a destination when I started driving." She paused, not wanting to reveal more. "I was tired and needed to stretch out a cramp, then I saw the bar. What does it matter?"

J.D. and Gabriel looked at each other, silent communication passing between them. Finally, J.D. spoke. "Hon, Blackstone is a shifter town."

"Shifter *town?*"

"Yeah, nearly everyone around here is a shifter," Gabriel said.

The air around them turned dead silent and Anna Victoria felt like someone had knocked her on the head. "You mean you guys are ..."

They both nodded.

Looking around, she saw a table with a family of four. "And them?"

Another double nod.

Rosie passed by and winked at them as she sat a couple at the next booth. "Her?"

"Yep," J.D. answered.

"Damon?" She didn't know why his name popped into her head, but somehow, she wanted to know.

"Yeah," Gabriel stated. "Most shifters come here because Blackstone is protected by a family of dragon shifters."

"Dragon?" *Oh goodness.* "I ... I ..." Her mind completely blanked. "I'm sorry ... I'm just ... I've only met maybe two or three shifters my entire life." And when she was younger, she had seen the videos of them changing into their animal forms. It was something she had done out of curiosity, because her other friends had done it, but she'd never looked at those videos again. It seemed like an incredible invasion of their privacy.

"It's all right," J.D. assured her. "I think we didn't realize that *you* didn't realize we were shifters. Most people who come here already know the deal."

"As you can imagine, this is just our normal everyday lives," Gabriel added.

*Except you turn into animals*, she added silently. "So, what are you guys?"

J.D.'s lips tightened, and her shoulders tensed. "It's actually rude to ask people that."

"Don't worry about J.D.," he smirked at the other woman.

"What she means is that *she's* the one who's sensitive about it. Care to take a guess what I am?"

"I wouldn't know where to start, honestly." And she didn't want to risk further offending either of them.

He chuffed. "I'm the king of the jungle, baby."

She sucked in a breath. "You're a lion?"

"Oh, yeah."

As he shook his long golden locks, Anna Victoria supposed it was an obvious guess. "I'm sorry, J.D., if I was being rude."

"It's all right." J.D. waved her hand casually. "But just be careful when you ask stuff like that around here."

Before anyone else could say anything, Rosie arrived holding a tray with their pies. "Here you go, kids." She placed the plates on the table. "Enjoy," she said before she walked to the next table.

J.D. lifted a forkful of apple pie into her mouth, chewed, then swallowed. "If you don't mind *me* being rude for a second, Anna Victoria, can I ask you where you're going?"

"I ... I don't know."

And now it all seemed to weigh on her. Yesterday, she'd been in survival mode, and the only thing she could think of was to get as far away from Albuquerque as possible.

"Do you have family elsewhere?"

She shook her head. "Anything and everything I know is back in New Mexico." And Edward Jameson's reach in the state was far and wide, which is why she high-tailed it out of there. He would not be happy being jilted at the altar *and* having his cash taken.

"So, what's your plan now?" J.D. asked.

She let out a long, deep sigh. "I don't know. Keep driving. North maybe." Colorado was still too close to New Mexico and Edward's influence. Canada might be far away enough, if she could manage to get a copy of her passport.

J.D. slapped a palm on the table. "I have an idea."

"You do?"

"Why don't you stay here?"

"What?" Searching her face, Anna Victoria could see J.D. was dead serious. "Where would I live? What would I do?"

"You can stay with me," J.D. declared. "I have a house and spare room."

"But I can't pay—"

"You can find a job here, something temporary, until you figure out what you want to do."

"I don't have a lot of work experience."

Actually, she had *zero*. She got her B.A. in Physical Education from NMU, but really, college was four years of partying, shopping, and going to brunch with her sorority sisters, thanks to her father's generous allowance. Afterwards, she moved back home, and her father had kept paying for everything—her phone, her car, her credit card balances. Why did she need to get a job when he footed the bill for everything?

As a parent, David Hall hadn't been affectionate while she was growing up. She suspected her mother's death had affected him a lot as he never remarried, and the fact that she was nearly a carbon copy of her made it difficult for him to even look at her. Still, no one could say he didn't provide for her. There had been nannies to look after her and chauffeurs to drive her everywhere. He paid for college and gave her anything and everything she asked for without reservations or without putting conditions that she get a certain degree, straight A's, or find a good job afterwards. At least, he didn't, until a few weeks ago. That night that changed her life.

She had come home after a day of shopping when he called her into his study. David Hall got up from behind his desk, whiskey glass in hand. It was obvious from the smell of liquor on his breath that he'd been drinking for a while.

"I'll get straight to the point, Anna Victoria," he had slurred. "We're ruined."

"Ruined? What do you mean?"

"I made some bad calls on some properties out east and ... it's gone. The money. The business. All gone. Or will be. Unless you do as I say." Apparently, he had borrowed a lot of money from the bank to cover his losses but they weren't enough. So he turned to alternative sources of cash, specifically, Edward Jameson, a prominent New Mexico "businessman". Jameson kept him afloat, but then the real estate market crashed ... and here she was.

*Maybe if I been more independent, I wouldn't be in this mess in the first place.*

"Anna Victoria?" J.D. waved a hand in front of her face.

"Oh. Sorry. Woolgathering," she confessed.

"Anyway," J.D. continued. "Why don't you check out my spare room first, and we can figure out a fair amount." Her mouth curled up into a smile. "Actually, I have a great idea. I know someone who needs some help at work. His last assistant just quit, and he needs someone to take up the slack while looking for a more permanent replacement."

Gabriel's eyebrows rose. "You can't mean—hey, what's that?" His nose wrinkled, and he sniffed the air. His gaze drew down to the table, his eyes narrowing at one of the plates in front of J.D. "Is that the hipster pie?"

"Hey!" J.D. cried out when Gabriel swiped the plate. "What are you doing?"

"It smells ... divine." His nose was so close to the pie that a spot of cream dotted the tip. "Trade you for a slice of pecan?" He looked at J.D. hopefully.

J.D. rolled her eyes. "It's already got your germs. Keep it." She turned back to Anna Victoria as Gabriel began to dig into the pie. "What do you say?"

"I don't—"

"Just come check out my place after we eat and think about it some more? What have you got to lose?"

Biting her bottom lip, Anna Victoria mulled it over. She supposed it wasn't a bad deal. Her only other option was to keep driving, but she could only get so far before she ran out of money. But J.D. was a complete stranger. "Could we get my keys and purse at The Den first?" If at least something felt off, she could just drive away.

"Sure, hon. And even if you don't decide to stay, how about I give your car a tune up before you leave? I own a garage in town, and I still want to make sure you're safe if you leave."

She sniffed. How was it possible these strangers were so nice? And they weren't even humans. The media often portrayed shifters as vicious and mean, with only the ones who do bad things getting any press.

"Th-thank you so much, I would appreciate that." A small weight had lifted off her shoulders. Her troubles were far from over, but it was a big deal that she could at least maybe have a place to stop and think about her future plans. "And thank you, too, Gabriel, for bringing me here."

Gabriel's eyes darted to the pie on her plate. "You can thank me by letting me swap your chai thingy for my cherry pie."

She laughed and pushed her plate at him. "Deal."

## Chapter 3

D amon let out a frustrated growl as he glanced at the folders on his desk. The pile seemed to mock him, but he couldn't ignore the growing stack anymore. *Damn reports.* He scrubbed a hand down his face.

They were supposed to be done two weeks ago, but he hadn't gotten around to them. Technically, his assistant was supposed to finish these reports and send them off, but since the last one quit and the staffing agency hadn't sent anyone else, it was up to him to get them done.

Pushing off from his desk, he wheeled his chair around to face the large windows that gave him an amazing view of the mountains and forests. The main Blackstone ranger station was located in the mountains, since most of the work involved anything and everything that had to do with the forests in the area. Their job involved most of the things normal forest rangers did in national parks—protect trails, wildlife, plants, and streams, and regulate the campsites.

However, there were two main differences between those parks and the Blackstone Mountains. First was that a main part of their job was to protect the shifters that called Blackstone home. Anyone who wanted to roam in their animal forms were free to do so in the public areas. But also, they had to watch out for anyone looking to cause trouble, which was why hunting of any kind was forbidden, and firearms and weapons were immediately confiscated.

The other part that set it apart from national forests and parks was the Blackstone Mountain was privately owned and operated by the Lennox Corporation, and not the federal or state government. That meant they only answered to one person: Matthew Lennox, current CEO of said corporation, and the dragon protector of Blackstone.

Which was why Damon was nearly drowning in paperwork. His reports kept Lennox Corporation up to date on their activities and ensured their funding flowed in. However, with his last assistant quitting and that damn blizzard last week, he was behind.

And now, the boss was coming in to see him. He'd actually forgotten about the meeting with being so busy and all. To think, he'd already been in a bad mood when he came in to the station this morning, and now that message from Lennox's assistant reminding him of this meeting was just the cherry on top of this shitshow.

And certainly, the events of last night and this morning didn't help.

When the woman in the wedding gown had passed out in his arms outside The Den, he couldn't even think of leaving her. The Demon had railed at him, swiping its claws at him, ready to fight if he even dared walk away from her. *As if I would leave any woman out there alone and defenseless.* Damon knew he was a bastard, but he wasn't a stupid one. So, he had no choice but to take her back to his place, tuck her into bed, and then spend a sleepless night tossing and turning on his couch as all he could think about was her.

*His mate.*

Anna Victoria.

Acting like an asshole to her this morning had been the right thing to do. It had driven her away, which was exactly what he wanted. The Demon disagreed and let its displeasure known, but he bore the pain because he couldn't risk getting close again. Not with anyone, and especially not with his own mate.

Yes, it was better if she left and drove far, far away from him and never saw him again. For her own sake.

A knock at the door made his spine stiffen. "Come in," he called as he twisted his chair around.

The door opened and a familiar face popped in. "Hey, Chief," Matthew Lennox greeted. "I'm here for our meeting."

He shot to his feet. "Mr. Lennox. Sir." Smoothing his hand down his khaki uniform shirt, he gestured to the chair. "Please, come in."

"C'mon, Damon, we went to high school together. You can call me Matthew, even at work," he said as he strolled in and took a seat.

Matthew Lennox had been in Damon's year back in high school, and though they had been in a few classes together, they hadn't run in the same social circles. Damon hung out with the jocks in the football team, and Matthew, well, he was a Lennox, after all, whose ancestor founded Blackstone. They were the richest family in town, and probably one of the wealthiest in the country.

Not that any of the Lennoxes were snobs, but they simply never had the chance to hang out outside school. Plus, Matthew was a dragon shifter, and even before his bear went out of control, Damon had been wary of his animal. As for the man himself, Matthew Lennox had always been cool, polite, and untouchable, probably because everyone knew he was being groomed to take over the billion-dollar corporation someday.

In recent years, however, Matthew's demeanor had warmed up, because he was now much more friendly and affable than he had been. Since Matthew had taken over as CEO a year or two ago, Damon had seen him at the Lennox Corporation picnics and Christmas parties, and he always took time to mingle and chat with everyone.

"How's it going, Chief?" Matthew leaned back in his chair, unbuttoning the coat of his expensive-looking suit. "That blizzard was terrible, huh?"

"Yeah, tell me about it. But we managed to round up all the campers and found all of the lost shifters caught in the storm."

"Good, good." The dragon shifter tapped his hands on the armchair. "How are you liking the job so far?"

Damon had been surprised that Matthew had picked him to replace the previous chief, Garret Simpson, who had retired after twenty years of service. He shrugged when Simpson had put his name in for the running, because surely, Matthew would see his record *and* read about his discharge from the Special Forces unit and pick someone else. But for some reason, Matthew *did* offer the position to him, with a review at the end of six months.

That's probably why he was here. Damon braced himself for any bad news Matthew was about to deliver. "Is this our formal performance review?" he asked. "Should I be getting ready to vacate this office?"

Matthew chuckled. "Always a straight shooter. I like that about you, Damon. Garret did, too, which was one of the reasons he put your name up when I asked him for a replacement."

"I'm sure the other candidates—"

"There were no other candidates."

"Excuse me?"

The dragon shifter leaned forward and rested his hands on

the table. Despite being on the other side of the desk, there was no question who was the more dominant creature here. "Damon, most people think the rangers have this cushy job, at least compared to the police and fire department. Like, all you guys do is muck around the forest and trails all day."

He huffed. Whenever all the Blackstone agencies got together, the rangers certainly got more than their fair share of the ribbing.

"I think not everyone understands how important your job is." Matthew's expression turned serious. "You protect the people of Blackstone when they're at their most vulnerable—sure, we may have some pretty vicious shifters around here who can hold their own, but there are also those who go out there to let their shifter side out, needing that time to themselves and not have to worry about getting lost, getting into accidents, or worse. The mountains are vital to the shifters of Blackstone, and you guys are the heart of this place."

"Huh." Damon was stunned. To him, being a ranger was a job—he liked doing it well enough, plus he could be outdoors, and more importantly, work in solitude. A "normal" job wouldn't have worked for him, not after what happened. But he'd never really thought of it the way Matthew put it.

"You say I'm a straight shooter," Damon began. "One of the reasons I became a ranger was because I need to be outdoors." He clenched his jaw. "I'm sure Garret told you about it."

Matthew nodded, but didn't say anything.

"Well, this job—being chief—has its perks, but being stuck inside just ain't me. And it ain't cutting it for my animal either." And that was one of the reasons he'd been even more frustrated the last couple of months. More responsibility, less time outdoors. No wonder he couldn't keep his anger in check.

"I see." Matthew tapped a finger on his chin. "Is that why your reports are always late?"

"Yeah, that, and I can't seem to stop my assistants from quitting." Okay, he knew he wasn't easy to work with. He liked things done a certain way, and it annoyed the shit out of him when people couldn't follow the simplest directions. But why the staffing agency kept sending him these timid little things that quit as soon as he lost his temper, he didn't know.

Matthew looked deep in thought. "Garret liked the leadership position because it allowed him to spend time on things he was good at, like managing the rangers, meeting with visitors and donors, and making everything run smoothly behind the scenes. You have a different working and leadership style, so really, this position can be what you make of it, as long as the work gets done at the end of the day. Maybe you need some help and—"

The door flew open, cutting Matthew off. Damon slammed his palm down. "Don't you fuckers ever knock—J.D.?"

J.D. McNamara blustered into his office with her usual no-nonsense, bulldozing personality. "Cooper, ya fartknocker, how's it—oh, didn't know you had company." Her gaze dropped to Matthew. "Hey, Matt, how's it hangin'? Can you let Catherine know her car's due for a tune-up?"

"J.D.," Matthew acknowledged. "I'll let my wife know, thank you for thinking of her."

J.D. owned the only garage in town so everyone took their vehicles to her for repairs and tune-ups. She also happened to be one of his oldest friends, along with Gabriel, and a general pain in his ass. If Gabriel had been his patient and silent support when he got back from the Army, J.D. was the one who pushed her way back into his life and bullied him until he snapped out of his funk. She never took no for an answer.

"So, how's it going, Damon?" she asked sweetly.

Damon frowned. J.D. was usually not this cheery this early in the morning unless she wanted something. "What is it?"

"Huh?" She perched her hip on the side of his desk, not really caring that he was already in the middle of a meeting with Matthew. "Can't I swing by and visit one of my oldest friends in the world, the one I've known since grade school, who I used to share my extra candy bars with?"

*Oh, she wanted something all right.* The only question now was what. "Spit it out, McNamara, so Matthew and I can finish our discussion."

"Oops." She put a hand over her mouth. "Sorry, Matt. Didn't realize you were in the middle of something."

Matthew smiled up at her, amused. "It's no trouble at all, J.D. I can wait."

"This'll only be a second." She turned back to Damon. "I know you fired your last assistant a couple weeks ago; what was her name? Claudine?"

"Justine," he corrected. "Claudine was the one before her."

"Well, it's hard to keep track. Anyway," she flashed him an extra sweet smile. "I have someone who can replace her. A friend of mine. Actually, she's going to be my new roommate."

"Roommate? You've never had a roommate before." J.D. lived in the same house she had grown up in and inherited, along with the garage, when her father passed away.

"Yeah, it's something I'm trying out," she said. "So, whaddaya say? She needs a job; you need an assistant."

Why did he have a feeling this wasn't what it seemed? "I don't know—"

"C'mon," she said. "She came all the way here to interview for the position."

"I'm not even taking candidates," he pointed out.

"You've been overworked and stressed." J.D. sighed. "Matthew, did you know that Damon didn't go home or even sleep during the entire blizzard? Gabriel says he had to practically shove food down his throat."

"Gabriel has a big fat mouth," he grumbled.

"Is that true, Damon?" Matthew asked. "I need my chief to be dedicated, but also alive and healthy."

"It's fine," he said. "I've been in worse situations."

"But this is what I'm talking about," Matthew said. "Some real help could be just what you need."

"I don't—"

"Why don't you show her in?" Matthew told J.D. "It's a long drive up here. If she came all the way, then she must really need a job."

"All right!" J.D. pumped her fist in the air. "She's right outside."

As J.D. disappeared through the door, Damon ran a hundred scenarios of who this person could be and what could happen. He was a planner, after all, and so he had to know what possible ways the enemy would react.

Of course, the person who did walk in through the door was the last person he expected.

*Her.*

Anna Victoria.

*Mine.*

The Demon roared in delight, seeing their mate. It had been cross the entire morning, ripping up at him from the inside when he let her go. When he fought back, the damned thing actually plunked down in the corner and sulked, seething at him. Now, that was definitely a first.

Anna Victoria was smiling when she entered his office, but when those large, pansy-blue eyes locked gazes with him, she grimaced. "What are you doing here?"

"Me?" He got up from his seat. "This is *my* office."

Her face went pale. "Y-your office?" Her head swung to J.D. "You said you knew someone who needed an assistant?"

"Yeah." J.D. jerked her thumb at Damon. "Him."

"I don't need an assistant," he groused. "And if I did, you'd be the last person I'd hire."

The look of hurt that crossed her face was unmistakable, and Damon felt his animal's claws drag down his insides. Why he said that, he didn't know, but he regretted it instantly. "I don't mean—"

It was too late. The door to his office slammed loudly, and she was gone. "Fuck." He raked his hands though his hair and sank back down on his chair.

"What the fuck did you say that for?" J.D. whacked her palm on his shoulder. "You didn't have to be so mean to her."

He was not going to play her games. "If that woman is your friend, I'll eat my hat." He knew everyone J.D. was friends with —and if Anna Victoria was one of them, she would have mentioned it this morning. "Did Gabriel put you up to this?"

"Damon Cooper, I know you've got issues, but can you for once *not* be an asshole?" J.D. crossed her arms over her chest and stamped a foot down. "That woman needs help. She's lost and scared and has nothing to her name."

"This morning, she didn't even know she was in Blackstone," he said. "And now she's staying? Doesn't that sound suspicious to you?"

"You're being paranoid, Damon," she said, not budging.

"She drove eight hours from New Mexico in a damned wedding gown and then stopped to get drunk at a bar," he pointed out. "And I'm the one who's crazy?"

"Please, Damon, won't you—"

"If you want her to have a job, you give her one." Let J.D. deal with that headache. Having her work here every damned day and be surrounded by her presence and scent—it would drive him bonkers.

The Demon, on the other hand, thought that was a very good idea.

"I don't need help," she said. "*You* do."

"Can we talk about this later? I'm in a meeting with—" Looking around, he saw that Matthew was not in the room. When did he slip out? "Goddammit." He couldn't believe it. His boss walked out on their meeting and now Damon had to worry about *his* job.

Pushing himself out of his chair, he dashed outside. *Maybe I'll catch him before he leaves.* Much to his relief, Matthew hadn't left the building yet. He was near the exit, but he wasn't alone. Anna Victoria was beside him, her face taut with despair. Matthew touched her shoulder and said something that made her expression relax.

Rage tore through him, and The Demon let out a deafening roar. How dare that male touch their mate? It didn't care that Matthew himself was already mated—or a dragon. Its lips drew back and its teeth bared, ready for a fight.

Damon wrestled for control, even though a part of him wanted to rip Matthew's hand away too. *A small part*, he told himself. *Very small.* When he calmed down enough, he managed to march toward the two, who were still chatting softly.

"Damon." Matthew's silver gaze locked onto him, and he frowned. It was like he could sense The Demon's anger. Being a shifter, he probably could.

"Apologies for the interruption." His teeth ground together so hard, it hurt. "We can continue our meeting or we can reschedule, whichever you prefer."

"I think our meeting is finished." The air around them turned cold as Matthew's silver gaze went steely. There was no mistaking the dominant power of his dragon. Even The Demon deferred to it, and slowly backed away.

His fists tightened at his side. And he thought this morning had been a shitshow. "All right. I suppose you'll want me out of the office by the end of the day?"

"What?" The atmosphere lightened again. "No, no. Jesus, Damon, I'm not going to fire you. I'd probably have a riot on my hands. Everyone here already respects you; they all had good things to say when my team did the reviews two weeks ago. I just came here to offer you the position permanently."

He swallowed. "Oh. I accept then." Frankly, if he did step down as chief, he wouldn't know what to do. It was unlikely he or The Demon would take orders from someone less dominant, and he really *would* have to quit.

"But ..."

Of course, there was a but.

"You'll need help, like I said." Matthew crossed his arms over his chest. "With an assistant, you can get more things done and spend less time at your desk. That's what you want isn't it?"

Yes, but he didn't want *her* as his assistant. He wouldn't be able to control himself, not with her around all the time. But it was obvious that Matthew had already made up his mind. "You got any experience?" he asked Anna Victoria.

Though her lower lip trembled, her shoulders straightened. "I was vice president of my sorority for two years. I basically had to do all filing and reports for the Dean's office, plus organize our mixers and events."

"And after you graduated?"

Her face turned red, and she swallowed. "I haven't really, er, worked since I graduated two years ago."

"It's a tough job market, amiright?" J.D. added, looking at Matthew and then Damon hopefully.

"You need an assistant, and she's here," Matthew said. "I won't tell you to hire her ..."

But he already knew the score. His boss wanted her here, and so, if he wanted to score points, he had to play nice. "Fine."

He ground his teeth. "You can start tomorrow. But on a probationary basis. Two weeks."

Her eyes lit up with hope and she smiled. "Thank you."

But she wasn't looking at him, rather, her gaze was on Matthew. And that annoyed the hell out of him. He only wanted her to smile for him.

*Where the hell did that thought come from?*

"She'll be here at nine," J.D. declared as she hooked her arm through Anna Victoria's. "C'mon. We should go and celebrate." With a final wave, she dragged Anna Victoria out the door.

Damon scrubbed a hand down his face. *I'm going to regret this.*

"Everything all right, Damon?" Matthew had the gall to ask.

Seeing as he didn't want to pick a fight this early in the day —and certainly not with a dragon—he merely returned the smile sarcastically. "Everything's fine, boss." Turning on his heel, he marched into his office and slammed the door.

# Chapter 4

Anna Victoria couldn't believe what just happened. When she walked into that office and saw *him*, she thought for sure she was going to have to leave town, which she would have hated. She'd only been in Blackstone for a day, but it was starting to grow on her.

After lunch, she and J.D. had parted ways with Gabriel and they went to The Den to pick up her car. Luckily, the owner, Tim, was already there and had kept her keys for her. Afterwards, they went to J.D.'s house, which was in a quiet little neighborhood on the east side of town.

Her place wasn't fancy, like her father's sprawling mansion back in Albuquerque, but it was spacious and clean. Anna Victoria liked that it felt homey and lived in, with various knickknacks, trophies, and photos of J.D. and her father on the walls.

The spare room wasn't large, but she did like that it had a sliding door and access to the wraparound deck and backyard. She was already planning on getting some plants and maybe a nice lounge chair so she could sunbathe in the back. Of course, that would all be dependent on if she could even get a job so she could pay for all this, which is why she was eager to meet this potential employer J.D. had told her about.

Well, Damon was not just a potential boss—he *was* her boss, at least starting tomorrow.

"What did I tell you?" J.D. said as they strolled out of the Blackstone Rangers headquarters. "That was easy-peasy, and now you can stay."

"Why didn't you tell me the job was to be *his* assistant?"

J.D. looked at her innocently. "What do you mean? I thought I mentioned it."

"No, you didn't," she said. "You said the job was assistant to the chief of the Blackstone Rangers."

"Who happens to be Damon," J.D. finished.

Unlinking her arm from the other woman's, she turned and faced J.D. "You know what I mean."

J.D. blew out a breath. "If I told you who it was, would you have come."

"Of course not." Why would she? He had been mean to her this morning, plus he'd seen her at her worst. Being around him would mean she would have to relive the most humiliating twelve hours of her life, under his glare.

"Then it's a good thing I didn't."

She opened her mouth then quickly shut it.

"Why did you accept the job if you didn't want to work with him?" J.D. asked.

"I ..." That was the question. "That other guy—Matthew—he seemed really nice. He spoke to me for a bit, and asked me if I was okay. He said he heard from you about my situation and was sympathetic. I just told him how much I liked Blackstone and really wanted to stay. Then you guys came and ..."

"It must be your lucky day," J.D. said with a chuckle.

"Why?"

"Because Matthew came to your defense. He's the boss

around here, and the Blackstone dragon doesn't just give everyone a chance, you know."

"The-the—what?" Matthew was a *dragon*? "Jeez."

"Don't worry, he's not going to eat you," J.D. assured her, as if that was something she said everyday. "And the fact that you have his stamp of approval means a lot."

"So, the only reason Damon hired me was because his dragon boss told him to do it?"

"And is that so bad? C'mon." J.D. dragged her to where her truck and the Mercedes were parked side-by-side. "Maybe you can find another job later. I mean, I'd hire you, but I, well ... no offense, but I'd guess you probably don't even know how to change your own tire."

"You'd guess right." She let out a long sigh. "I guess I'll have to just take it one day at a time." Frankly, she was glad she could stay; with no other prospects, she could only go so far, even with the cash in the trunk of her car. At some point, she might have to go back to her father. At least tomorrow she'd have a job and a paycheck in two weeks.

Who knows, maybe working for Damon wouldn't be so bad?

———

"You can do this," Anna Victoria said, giving herself a little pep talk as she stood outside the Blackstone Rangers headquarters.

She wiped her sweaty palms down the front of the blouse and black jeans she'd borrowed from J.D. While there was still some cash leftover in her wallet after buying some groceries, she would still need to make do with what clothes J.D. could lend her until she got her paycheck. It should be enough to afford some basics she could mix and match. Then maybe if things went well, she could also get some other luxuries, like makeup.

For now, the lipstick and powder she kept in her purse would have to do.

The large wood and stone building that served as the headquarters of the Blackstone Rangers was exactly what she imagined it would be—rustic and functional, but it perfectly fit the surroundings. It was a long drive into the mountains, but as she got deeper into the forest, she could see the appeal of being out here—everything seemed fresh and the mountain views were beautiful. J.D. did caution her about driving up the steep roads, but she didn't exactly have much of a choice, so she drove her Mercedes up carefully. There was still snow piled up on the side, probably from that big blizzard everyone kept talking about.

With another deep breath, she pushed on the heavy wooden door and let herself in. It looked like any typical office she supposed, except that everyone was wearing khaki uniforms, hats, and boots. Oh, that, and everyone around here was *hot*.

Now, she was no stranger to good-looking men. After all, she was part of Pi Beta Kappa, one of the most popular sororities on campus, and thus had her pick of all the cute college boys, from the football jocks to frat bros. However, these guys seemed like a whole new level. Everyone was over six feet tall, built like lumberjacks, and strutted around with a confident and magnetic air about them. Even the one or two female rangers she spied were also fit and gorgeous. In some of her biology classes, they'd briefly touched on shifter physiology and how they were faster and stronger than humans, and they also healed quickly and hardly got sick. But, none of her books or professors talked about how outrageously attractive shifters were.

And then there was Damon. For some reason, most of her thoughts kept coming back to him. Although everyone around here was attractive, there was just something about him that she found unforgettable. Maybe it was those soulful brooding green eyes of his.

*Brooding?* She scoffed at herself. But still, she couldn't help but think of his broad shoulders and that tight T-shirt and wondered if his chest was smooth underneath or hairy ...

*Oh, stop.*

Thinking those thoughts would not end well. Despite all the guys who chased after her throughout college, she always ended up with the ones who treated her like trash and broke her heart. Why couldn't she be attracted to the nice guys, like Gabriel? Even now, her stomach fluttered at the thought of being *near* Damon.

"Hey, baby, whatcha looking for? Or should I ask, *who?*"

She stiffened and whirled around. A man stood behind her, a cocky grin on his face and his golden eyes sparkling. Like everyone around here, he, too, was amazingly gorgeous. And from his smirk, he knew it. "I'm—"

"Get lost, Anders. She's not interested."

She exhaled in relief when she saw who it was. "Hey, Gabriel," she greeted, glad to see him here.

"Hey, Anna Victoria," he greeted back. "So, I take it you got the job?"

"How do you know?" They hadn't seen each other or spoken since yesterday, and J.D. didn't mention anything about working here.

"I, er, kinda guessed," he said sheepishly. "When J.D. mentioned that friend who needed an assistant."

"How do you know this angel from heaven?" The other man wiggled his brows at her.

"Oh, brother." She rolled her eyes. "Don't you have anything more original than that?"

His smile widened. "So, what you're saying is, I should try harder?"

55

Gabriel whacked him on the shoulder. "Lay off. She's the chief's new assistant."

"Temporarily," she added. "I'm on probation for the next two weeks."

"Isn't that nice? Anna Victoria, was it?" Anders's golden gaze flickered over her. "Well, the name's Anders Stevens. If you need me to show you the ropes, just holler. I can do other things with ropes too—ow!"

That earned him another smack on the head. "You're a walking sexual harassment suit, you know that?"

Anders tsked. "You're certainly prettier than the last ones. I hope you last longer than them." Anders flashed her another flirtatious grin before laughing and walking away.

Gabriel steered her away. "Sorry about that," he said. "He's mostly harmless. And not everyone around here is as unprofessional as him."

"Wait, what does he mean 'the last ones'?"

"Er ..." He looked sheepishly at the floor. "Damon's gone through quite a number of assistants in the last six months."

"A number? How many?"

"About eight."

"Eight?" she exclaimed. "Does he gobble them up?"

"Not literally," he said. "But ... he's got a special way of working. But don't worry, his bark is worse than his bite. Most of the time I mean."

She worried her lip. However, she was determined to make this work. "I'm tougher than I look."

"I hope so," he chuckled. "Since you're going to be dealing with Damon all day."

"Is that supposed to make me feel better?"

"No, just to prepare you." He shook his head. "I don't know what J.D. was thinking."

"I don't either but ... I just need this job." The more she

thought about it, she realized what an idiot she'd been, just driving off without a plan. If she hadn't driven into Blackstone or met J.D., who knows where she'd have ended up? Right now, Blackstone was her only option.

"It's all right," he soothed, placing a hand on her arm. "I'm sure you'll do great."

Someone clearing their throat made her start. Standing in the doorway of the office was the man himself. And for some reason, he looked *pissed*.

Gabriel stepped back and put his hand down. "Morning, Chief," he greeted.

Damon let out a grumble, then turned to her. "There's your desk. You know your way around a computer, I assume. The inbox on the desktop is yours, clear it out. I'll send you instructions there." He disappeared into his office without another word.

Her hands balled into fists at her side. Not even a welcome or good morning. *How rude.*

"Don't worry about him," Gabriel said reassuringly. "He's just ... well, that's just the way he is."

"And what's that? A *b-hole*?" Okay, so maybe it wasn't a great idea to call the boss names on her first day, especially if said boss had super senses. "Oh God, do you think he heard me say that?"

He chuckled. "Nah, a bear's hearing isn't as good as a feline's."

*Huh.* So, Damon was a bear shifter. It kind of made sense, seeing as he was so grumpy all the damned time.

Gabriel patted her on the shoulder reassuringly. "Listen, my shift's about to start soon. But I can swing by for lunch. We can eat in the cafeteria, since you brought your own." He glanced down at the brown paper bag in her hand.

"That would be nice. Thanks."

"You'll do great," he said with a wave as he walked away. "I'll see you soon."

When Gabriel was out of sight, she turned back to her desk. It was bare and clean, except for the phone, computer screen, and keyboard. Planting herself on the chair, she booted up the machine and waited for the screen to light up. Once it did, she opened the flashing mail icon on the desktop.

The message notification sound pinged, one right after the other and soon, the inbox was bursting with new emails. Seeing as Damon said it was hers, she clicked on the oldest unopened email from a few weeks back. It was some kind of advertisement from a clothing company, so she quickly junked that.

It took her about an hour to remove all the spam mail and unsubscribe the inbox from various email newsletters. The previous user of this inbox obviously loved online shopping. *Who the heck uses company email for personal use?* Even with her non-existent work experience, she knew better than that.

Now to tackle all the official-looking emails. First, she went through the oldest ones. Mostly it looked like requests and questions from employees and the general public. She categorized them for now since she really didn't know how to answer them. Maybe she could ask Damon.

Apprehension filled her as she glanced at the door to his office. But what else was she supposed to do? He didn't exactly leave her any instructions. She stood up from her desk and circled around to head into his office.

"Uh, Damon?" she asked, peeking her head through the doorway.

His head whipped toward her. "Don't you know how to knock?"

The gruffness in his voice made her pull her head back. After a deep breath, she knocked on the door and poked her head through again. "Damon?"

Now he was scowling at her. "That's not what I—never mind. What do you want?"

*Did the man go through his day trying to find new ways of being unpleasant?* Walking inside, she stopped in front of his desk. "I just wanted to know what you want me to do with the unread emails that aren't junk or spam. I was cleaning out the general inbox and I have about twenty or thirty emails that need attention."

His frown deepened. "Who told you to do that?"

"You did," she huffed. "You said clear it out."

"And I also told you that I would be sending you instructions on what needs to be done," he said, irritated. "I've sent you six emails. What have you been doing the hour and a half?"

Her lips pursed together. "I was working the older emails since some of them have been sitting there for weeks."

"Are you the boss, or am I?"

God, what was up with this man? "You are. I'll get right on it," she said curtly, then turned around and marched outside.

*You need this job*, she said to herself after taking a long, cleansing breath. It was this or going back to her father and Edward. Just thinking about *that* made Damon's rudeness tolerable. *Almost.*

She sat back down and opened the newest six emails, all from Damon. Each one had a curt line or two, telling her what to do with the attached files. No "please" or "thank you" or even a "kind regards." No, it was just "print this leave it in my inbox" or "proofread and forward to HR."

Cracking her knuckles, she went right to work. Truly, it wasn't difficult, but she could see why his last eight assistants quit. Not everyone needed their hand held or back patted all the time, but he could at least make the effort to be polite, like a normal human being.

But he wasn't a normal human being. Damon was a bear shifter. The thought of him turning into a large furry beast made her shiver.

Finally, it was lunch time, and there were only two more emails from Damon she hadn't yet opened and worked on. But that could wait. Surely, a one-hour noon break was allowed.

"Hey, Anna Victoria!"

Swiveling her seat around, she saw Gabriel approaching her. He wasn't alone though, as a tall, blond man walked beside him. As expected, he, too, was fit and good-looking. "This is Daniel Rogers," he introduced. "Don't worry, he's the nicest guy around here."

"Pleased to meet you." Daniel's blue eyes twinkled. "And please, Gabriel's exaggerating about being the nicest around here."

"Yeah, well she met Anders first thing this morning," Gabriel said, rolling his eyes.

She offered her hand, which Daniel shook. "Pleased to meet you, too, Daniel." His grip was strong, but friendly.

"Ready for lunch?" Gabriel asked.

She glanced quickly at the door to Damon's office, then shrugged. "Yeah." Standing up, she grabbed her water bottle and brown paper bag that contained her tuna sandwich. "Let's go."

The two guys led her to the "cafeteria" in the back of the building, which was unlike any lunchroom she'd ever seen. For one thing, it was more like an outdoor picnic area surrounded by tall pine trees and an amazing view of the snowcapped mountains in the distance.

"Wow," she exclaimed as she sat down on one of the benches. "Some cafeteria."

"Working here certainly has its perks," Daniel said.

Gabriel sidled up next to her. "Yeah, you get used to it."

"Five years working here, and you still can't appreciate nature." Daniel shook his head.

"I like nature well enough, but I'm not going to roll around in it and pretend it's the best thing ever," he shrugged. "Anyway, why don't you go and grab some food, and I'll keep Anna Victoria company?"

As Daniel nodded in agreement and walked toward the counter, Gabriel turned to her. "So, how was your morning?"

She blew out a breath, sending a stray lock of hair in her eyes flying. "I wish I could say it was good, but you did warn me." She relayed what happened with Damon. "It's like he hates me."

"No way," he protested. "I mean ... he's like that with most people."

"So, he just hates everyone, not me in particular?"

"Er ..." He tugged at the collar of his uniform. "I guess. But if you knew him better, you'd understand."

"You're his friend, right? So why does he act like ... like ..."

"An asshole?"

She chuckled. "Yeah."

"He's—"

"I'm back." Daniel slid onto the bench seat in front of her. "Your turn, Russel."

"You know, you guys could have gone together," she pointed out. The lion shifter merely waved a hand as he walked away.

"So, Anna Victoria," Daniel began. "Gabriel tells me you were the one in the dress at The Den the other night."

She groaned. "You were there, too?"

He nodded. "Afraid so. But we don't have to talk about that, if you don't want to."

"Thanks," she said. "So, do you like working as a ranger?"

"Yeah, I enjoy it...."

Anna Victoria listened to Daniel talk, glad to not have to tell him more about herself or her situation. Gabriel joined them soon after and added to the conversation.

As lunch went on, she found herself having a good time, even forgetting about that morning's debacle. She enjoyed the company of the two men, though she did find it strange that they warded off anyone who tried to approach them, except for the two female rangers who had introduced themselves to Anna Victoria.

"You're too skinny," Gabriel said as he dropped his plate of fries in front of her. "Eat."

"Skinny?" she said. "I'll have you know, I run a six-minute mile, and I've been doing the New Mexico Breast Cancer Marathon every year for the last three years." While she wasn't an elite athlete, she did enjoy exercising and staying fit. Aside from running, she did yoga, aerobics, Pilates, and barre. "Besides, I can't eat trash like that and not have it go straight to my hips."

"You're not a vegetarian, are you?" Gabriel teased.

"If I was, you'd know it," she snorted. "I—"

"What's going on here?"

Gooseflesh rose on her arms. Turning around, she found a pair of clear green eyes boring into her. There was no mistaking the stern expression on Damon's face.

"Hey, Chief," Daniel greeted. "Just having lunch. Have you eaten?"

"I said, what's going on here?" he repeated, his eyes never leaving hers.

"I'm just having lunch," she said. "Is there a problem with that?"

"You're five minutes late." He cocked his head toward the large clock on the wall.

"Oh. Right." Her cheeks heated. "I'm sorry about that. It won't happen again."

"See that it doesn't."

"Damon. *Dude.*" Gabriel got up and stood toe-to-toe with him. "It was five minutes. We got a little carried away. It's no big deal."

"Aren't you late for your shift too?" he asked, stretching out to full height, which was two inches taller than Gabriel.

"It's fine, Gabriel." She quickly gathered her trash and her purse. "I'll head back to my desk now." The tension in the air was too much, and she couldn't wait to get away from there, so she slung her purse over her shoulder, stomped over to the trash can, and tossed her rubbish into it.

Hands balled at her sides, she took deep breaths to relieve the tightness in her chest. Why the heck was Damon such a jerk? Sure, she was late, but he could have been nicer about reminding her. Did he stalk all the way to the cafeteria to drag her back to her desk?

"Anna Victoria, wait up!" Gabriel shouted as she walked back into the building.

Though she was tempted to keep walking, it wouldn't have worked because he caught up to her, blocking her way. "Sorry about that," he said.

She sniffed. "You have nothing to be sorry for."

"Damon—"

"Yeah, yeah, I know. That's just the way he is with everyone. I shouldn't take it so personally. But he ... he just makes it so difficult." Her fists tightened even more. "Maybe I should just quit. He didn't want me here in the first place."

"Quit? Are you crazy?" Gabriel gripped her shoulders. "Listen to me, Anna Victoria, you can't let him get to you. The more you shrink back, the worse it will be. Just stand up to him if it's too much; he'll back down. Besides, do you really want to leave Blackstone?"

She sighed. "No." *I can't give up now.* J.D. and Gabriel had put in a lot of effort to help her and make her welcome. "I'll just ... try harder I suppose."

"That's the spirit." He clapped her on the shoulder. "You'll do great. I know it."

When she looked behind him, she saw Damon walking up to them. The look on his face was, not friendly, but less severe. Maybe it was even remorseful.

"Anna Victoria, I—" His mouth clamped shut when his gaze landed on Gabriel's hand resting on her shoulder. His expression turned dark again, then he turned on his heel and headed in the opposite direction.

*I don't understand him.* And maybe she never would. But she didn't need to. All she had to do was survive the next two weeks.

## Chapter 5

Damon wasn't sure how he managed to survive five days being around Anna Victoria. It had been pure torture, seeing her every day, sitting at the desk outside his office. His damned bear wouldn't let up either. The Demon wanted him to go after her, claim her and take her, to keep all the other males from sniffing around her. After the third day, he started coming in earlier and leaving when he knew she was long gone, just to evade her presence.

Of course, he couldn't completely avoid her. She came in several times to his office to ask questions and give him paperwork to sign. When she did come in, he did his best to be cold and distant. He regretted reprimanding her for being five minutes late during her lunch hour that first day, but it was all he could do to stop The Demon from ripping off Gabriel and Daniel's heads for daring to be near her. After calming himself down, he did go back to apologize, but seeing Gabriel with her just made him burn with jealousy. Even now, things were not quite right between him and his best friend, but he couldn't bring himself to tell him why he was acting like an asshole.

So, for now, he decided to just keep things cold and

professional. Even if all he wanted to do when she came into his office was bend her over his desk and bury himself in her.

He raked his fingers through his hair in frustration. He hadn't even wanted sex in a very long time. *No.* He couldn't risk it again. Staying away was the best thing. For her own safety.

A ringing sound jolted him out of his thoughts. Reaching for his phone, he answered it. "Cooper."

"Chief, this is Mathers. I need you to check something out in sector Two-A."

Normally, he would tell whoever it was to fix it on their own because he wasn't a micromanager, but it would be a good excuse to get out of here—and away from Anna Victoria. "All right. Give me five, and I'll be there."

Getting up from his desk, he marched out of his office, already focusing his gaze away from Anna Victoria's desk. The plan was to avoid eye contact or any contact. At least, it was until he saw Harry Wolford, one of his rangers, leering at Anna Victoria's bust. The top two buttons of her blouse were open, and whenever she leaned forward to answers questions, her breasts would push together.

"Wolford!" he barked.

Wolford's body went straight at attention, and he turned around, his eyes widening. "Ch-Chief!"

"If you'd pay attention to anything else but tits and ass, maybe you'd get your patrol done on time!"

"Y-yes, Chief. Sorry about that! I'll get right on it, sir!" Wolford made an about-face and scampered away.

"You didn't have to shout at him," Anna Victoria berated. Her lower lip trembled, and he had to admit, she had balls to talk back to him even though he could clearly smell the nerves rolling off her. "He didn't do anything. We were just talking."

The fact that another male even dared talked to her was

enough to rile him and The Demon up. "Perhaps next time, you can dress more appropriately, Ms. Hall."

"Dress appropriately?"

He nodded to her blouse. "Wearing stuff like that won't score you any brownie points around here."

Her hands went to her chest, and her face went red as a fire engine. "I—excuse me." She swallowed hard, got up from the chair, and spun on her heels.

He didn't miss the way her hands shook or how her blue eyes went shiny with unshed tears, but he couldn't do anything but watch her walk away. The Demon roared at him, furious that he made their mate cry.

"Goddammit!" he roared back as he marched into his office and slammed the door behind him. "Motherfucker!" He wanted to destroy something. To rip up the walls and furniture with his claws, whatever it took to get out this frustration of being so near the one person he craved, but couldn't have.

"Damon, what the fuck?"

He had been so consumed with his anger that he didn't hear the door open. Letting out a snarl, he spun on his heels. Of course, it was Gabriel. "What do you want?"

Gabriel was an easygoing and laid-back person. He couldn't remember the last time he'd seen his best friend angry, so it was a surprise to see his face red with fury, the muscles in his neck straining. "What the fuck did you say to her this time? She was near tears when I saw her."

"Leave it alone, Gab," he said, full warning in his voice. "You do *not* want to mess with me right now."

"Is that so?" He could feel Gabriel's lion, raring for a fight. "Maybe it'll help knock some goddamn sense into you."

"Try me, Russel, just fucking try."

"Jesus, Damon, are you hearing yourself right now?" Gabriel said. "What the hell is the matter with you? You weren't this much of an asshole to your other assistants. Why are you so determined to punish that girl when she's done nothing to you?"

Gabriel was right, he knew that. And his last remarks to her had been personal and uncalled for. But he couldn't help himself. The Demon's temper was always difficult to control, but when it came to their mate, it was utterly unmanageable. It hated Damon right now because he hurt her, and he hated Gabriel for the friendship they had formed in the last week. "Are you trying to screw her, is that it?"

"Fuck you, Cooper," Gabriel shouted. "It's not about that, and you know it." Anger rolled off him in waves. "Please do us all a favor around here and spend your weekend pulling your head out of your ass!"

Goddammit, he couldn't believe he said that to Gabriel. His best friend. "Gabe, I'm so—"

"Save it." He raised his hands and then spun around and marched out of his office.

Fucking hell, this wasn't what he wanted. He didn't want to fight with one of the few friends he had left. But he didn't have a clue how to fix all this. Maybe this was for the best, and he was meant to be alone all his life to atone for the sins of his past.

———

After Damon responded to the call from Mathers, he decided not to go back to HQ. Instead, he stayed out, patrolled a couple of sectors that he knew would be empty and came back when he was sure Anna Victoria and most of the people on day shift would have gone home. It was Friday night after all, and for most normal people, that meant a relaxing weekend ahead.

When was the last time he had any time to relax? He couldn't remember. Though he was technically off on Saturday and Sunday, he still checked in at the station on weekends or caught up with paperwork. Being alone with his animal was never relaxing, and he needed the distraction.

Taking his hat off, he wiped the sweat from his brow as he entered the station. To his surprise, the lobby wasn't empty. J.D. was there, leaning on the front desk.

"Well, look what the cat dragged in," she said, smirking.

"Shouldn't I be saying that about *you*?"

J.D. grimaced. He knew she *hated* talking about her animal. As far as he knew, only he and Gabriel knew the true nature of her shifter side. "Where've you been?"

"Out. We're shorthanded today, so I went patrolling. Is there a reason you're here?"

She frowned. "You forgot, didn't you?"

"Forgot what?"

"What day it is?"

"What day?" His tried to recall the date, but since last week, the days seemed to meld together. Then he remembered. "Jesus." He blew out a breath. "J.D. I'm sorry. I truly am. I forgot ... about today." He'd been so busy and distracted, he forgot today was her father's birthday. The old man had been gone over ten years now, but to J.D., it was a sacred day. Jimmy McNamara had loved birthdays, after all and he never forgot anyone's, plus he always had a party on his day. "Every year you're still alive is a reason to celebrate," he had always said.

"Are you ready to go then?" J.D. asked.

Every year, except for when he was deployed, they would go down to The Den and have drinks until J.D. would get so drunk, she'd pass out. It was a kind of tradition, a way they remember the old man. It was really the only night he would endure being in a crowded place like The Den. The last few years it hadn't been so bad because it was always a weekday. It was just his luck that this time around it fell on a Friday.

"I'm sorry, J.D. I can't." There was no way he was going to

be able to control The Demon, not tonight. "I'll make it up to you, I swear."

"You *can't*?" she hissed. "You haven't even stepped foot into The Den. You can't back out, Damon." Her voice trembled. "Not now. Not tonight."

J.D. *never* cried except when it was about her old man. He had raised her alone since her mom died, and they had been close as could be. "J.D.—"

"Please. I need you there."

He growled inwardly. *Just for tonight*, he told his animal, *behave*. Maybe this year, J.D.'d get drunk faster, then he could go home. "Let me get ready, okay?"

Ten minutes later, after showering and getting dressed, he was driving down the mountain road, following J.D. in his truck. When they pulled up into The Den's parking lot, it was nearly full which meant the inside would be packed.

Cutting off the engine, he took a deep breath. He realized he didn't even ask about Gabriel. The lion shifter would be there of course; Gabriel would never forget such an occasion. Hopefully they could put their anger aside for tonight, for J.D.

He hopped out of his truck and headed toward the entrance. J.D. was already there, waiting for him.

"I do appreciate you coming. Despite, you know." She nodded at the door.

He could already hear the noise coming from the inside. "I might have to make an early exit, but why don't I buy you two bottles tonight, and you can drink yourself silly faster?"

She laughed. "Deal."

He held the door open, and then followed her in. The moment he stepped inside, the noise, the heat, and the crowd made his chest tighten. The Demon roared to life, clawing at him. *Calm down.* He wasn't sure if he was talking to himself or his animal.

"We got a place reserved, don't worry," J.D. assured him and nodded to where the billiard room was located. There was a signboard in front of it that said, "Reserved for a Private Event."

"Wow," he said. "I didn't think Tim ever closed off a portion of The Den."

"Yeah well, you know him and Dad. They were tight." She waved to Tim as they walked by the bar, who acknowledged them with a nod.

It seemed like an eternity before he reached the billiard room, but finally he stepped inside. In here, he breathed easier, and his anxiety levels lowered. He recognized a few of the old-timers from J.D.'s garage, the ones who had worked with the old man. And of course, Gabriel was there, in the corner, holding a drink. They exchanged glances, a silent message passed between them to put their unfinished business aside for now for their friend's sake.

"Here you go," Gabriel handed him and J.D. a glass of bourbon each, which had been her father's drink of choice.

"Thanks," he replied, trying to keep his voice neutral as he didn't want J.D. to notice things between him and Gabriel were strained.

"To the old man," Gabriel said, raising his glass.

They followed suit, and J.D. downed hers in one go, then handed her keys to Gabriel. "You still driving me home?"

"Can we have a pajama party after?" he asked cheekily, which earned him a playful slap on the shoulder. The lion shifter wasn't being serious of course; they'd been friends for so long that it would be weird to be anything more than that.

"Thanks," he said as Gabriel refilled his glass.

"Let's get everyone to toast to him." Gabriel went around, gathering people so he could pour them some liquor.

"You okay?" Damon asked J.D.

"Yeah." J.D.'s personality was like a hurricane—she

bulldozed anything in her path, which was why most people found her abrasive and loud. However, this was one of the few times she was subdued. "This day is always, you know. Tough. I —oh, she's here!"

Every nerve ending in Damon's body lit up, as if he already knew *who* was here. He turned to the entrance, and sure enough, it was Anna Victoria. Though she was wearing the same blouse and pants as earlier, she had her hair down around her shoulders, and her lips were red and glossy. She was smiling as she entered, but when their gazes locked, her smile evaporated.

"What is *she* doing here?" he asked, fingers curling tightly around the glass.

"She's my friend and roommate," J.D. stated. "I invited her. Why, what's wrong?"

"Nothing." The fact that J.D. didn't know anything told him that neither Anna Victoria nor Gabriel told her about how he'd acted this week and this afternoon. If she did, J.D. would surely have torn him a new one by now. "I should go get that second bottle for you."

He slunk away in shame. Anna Victoria could easily have swayed J.D. to her side by telling her how he'd been a damn asshole this week, but she didn't. Not liking the guilt seeping into him, he swiftly headed to the bar and asked Tim for a bottle of bourbon. After paying, he headed back to the billiards room, carefully watching Anna Victoria from the corner of his eye to make sure he stayed away. The Demon did not like that one bit, but he was in charge here.

As the night wore on, J.D. got drunker, as expected. It was clear that even after all this time, she still keenly felt the loss of her father. He couldn't even imagine what that was like—after all, his own parents were still alive, living down in Florida after his father retired from working in the Blackstone mines most of his life. He called them regularly, on birthdays and holidays, saw them when they came for visits, but he knew he could do better. It was just difficult to connect with them again, after all that happened.

"You about ready to go home?" he asked J.D.

"Naw," she slurred. "I ain't no quitter!" It took a hell of a lot of liquor to get a shifter drunk, and everyone had been buying drinks for her all night. "But ... I should go to the bathroom."

"Do you need help?"

"Pffft!" She waved him away. "I'll get Anna Victoria to go with me."

He watched as J.D. went to Anna Victoria, who was chatting with Gabriel and a few of the older guys from the garage. The two women linked arms and then headed out of the billiards room. When she was out of his sight, an uncomfortable feeling settled in his chest and he couldn't tear his eyes away from the door, wondering when they'd be back.

A few minutes later, J.D. returned, but Anna Victoria wasn't with her. His beast clawed at him, urging him to find out where she was.

"You're back," he said to J.D. "By yourself."

"Yeah. So, what's wrong with that?"

"I thought Anna Victoria went with you?"

"She said she was going to ask Tim for a drink of water," J.D. said with a shrug. "Did you—"

Not bothering to wait for her to finish, he marched toward the main room. It was even more crowded now, and he stopped suddenly, as if an invisible barrier hit him.

*Too many people.*

*Too noisy.*

*Hot, too hot.*

*Moving.*

*Feet stamping.*

*Pain.*

He let out a soft growl and shook himself out of the daze. With a deep breath, he scanned the room. Sure enough, there she was at the bar. But she wasn't alone. Some guy was chatting her up already.

*Goddammit.* She was too damn beautiful for her own good. Gritting his teeth, he marched over to the bar, not even caring about the heat and noise and the crowd.

"... I don't think I've seen anyone as pretty as you around here," the man said, sidling closer to Anna Victoria. Damon recognized him as one of the firemen from Blackstone F.D. He smelled feline, probably mountain lion.

"I just moved here and—" Her mouth clamped shut when her eyes landed on Damon. Blonde brows drew together, and she moved aside, even closer to that asshole. "Go ahead," she said, motioning to the empty space at the bar.

He couldn't say anything, so he just continued to stare at her.

She rolled her eyes. "Fine," she said, then turned back to the man next to her. "As I was saying ..."

Her dismissive attitude and the way she smiled at that other man made hot, searing jealousy roll up tight in his chest. "I don't need a drink."

Exasperated, she turned to him. "Then what *do* you need?"

Oh, he was going to show her what he needed all right. Without another word, he hooked his arm through hers and dragged her away from the bar. She let out a yelp, but he ignored her. When that bastard fireman tried to protest, he shot him a look that said, *just try it*, and the other man quickly backed away.

Despite her protests, he managed to maneuver her outside. The cold, biting air was a welcome respite from the stuffiness and noise inside.

"What the *heck*!" Anna Victoria screeched, disentangling her arm from his. "You ... you ... knucklehead! What do you think you're doing?" Her chest heaved as she struggled to take in big gulps of air. "Wasn't it enough that you humiliated me in front of other employees, but you have to do it out here too? You can't control who I speak to when I'm on my personal time."

His fists tightened at his sides. "You didn't even know who that was."

"That's what you do in bars, get to know people," she huffed. "Are you determined to make me miserable and ensure I never make friends? Did you want to isolate me so that I leave Blackstone?"

"Goddammit, that's not what—"

"Then what the heck did you do that for?"

"That guy, and any guy in there, they aren't looking to be your friend."

"Ha!" She raised her hand in frustration. "I'm not a child, you know! And so what? I'm not allowed to have any *friends*? Who else am I supposed to be friends with, you?"

"I don't want to be your friend," he gritted out.

"That's obvious. I—"

What he should have done was walk away. But instead, he gripped her by the arms and pushed her against the wall, caging her in. He couldn't take it. She was driving him crazy, and it needed to stop.

"D-Damon?"

Wide pansy-blue eyes looked up at him. But he couldn't smell fear on her. Only ... excitement? He could hear her heart beating fast, smell her sweet scent, and read the confusion play across her face at the conflicting emotions.

"What are you doing?"

He didn't know. Didn't care. Except he had to have her. Leaning down, he brushed his lips against hers. She tensed, but only for a moment, before relaxing against him, and soon, she was kissing him back too.

God, he'd never had anything as sweet as her lips. He licked his tongue out to swipe at those lush petals, making her moan and part her mouth. Tentatively, he brushed inside her mouth, past her teeth, to touch his tongue with hers.

One hand moved up to her neck, caressing the soft skin there, making her moan into his mouth. The Demon roared, wanting him to do more. Take her. Claim her. Black claws extended from his fingers and he raked them gently down to her collarbone. She didn't seem to notice as she was eagerly opening her mouth to him, her tongue dancing against his. His cock hardened instantly in his jeans, straining against the seam so hard it was painful.

His claws moved lower, to that damned blouse. She had buttoned it up all the way, maybe because of what he said. In any case, it wouldn't stand a chance against him. He slipped his claws between the slit in the front and snipped the buttons off, one by one, until her skin was bared to the cool evening air.

Then another set of memories flooded into his brain.

*The Demon slipping from his control.*

*Muscles stretching and contracting.*

*Claws ripping out.*

*A scream.*

"No!" He snarled and pushed away from her. "I can't ..." *Not again.* The air in his lungs rushed out, leaving an ache in his chest. *Slow breaths. Slow breaths.* The oxygen slowly returned, and he pushed those memories away. "I ... Anna Victoria ..."

To his surprise, she didn't run away right then and there. But she was still pushed up against the wall, her hands clutching her ruined blouse together.

"Fuck!" he growled. No, he couldn't do this. Not to *her* of all people. "Damn you!" he said to The Demon. "Ruined my life

..." He glanced back at her again, and this time, he could smell the fear from her. *See what you did? You can't keep doing this!*

His animal roared back in protest, and pressed its claws at him.

*I'm a bastard.* It wasn't supposed to be this way. Life was unfair, he knew that, but he hadn't hated how unfair it was until this moment. To have what he wanted within reach, but knowing he could never have it.

The Demon clawed at his skin from the inside, and he knew there was no turning back now. "Get away!" he screamed at her. "Go!"

She let out a yelp, then ran past him. He wanted to follow her, make sure she was okay, but it wouldn't be safe. So, he ran in the opposite direction, through the line of trees, making it just in time before The Demon tore out of him.

# Chapter 6

Anna Victoria tossed in bed for what seemed like the thousandth time. She had tried everything to fall asleep— a hot bath, drank some milk, counted sheep—but nothing worked. Her mind refused to shut down, and her body ... well, it was like it had never felt more alive after Damon touched her.

*I shouldn't have gone to the party.*

But J.D. had invited her to go, and since it had been a long week, she deserved some R and R. It seemed strange to celebrate the birthday of someone who had passed away, but she understood that you never really got over losing a parent. Her own mother had died of breast cancer when Anna Victoria was only ten years old.

Besides, J.D. said it was only going to be a few people who had been close to her father, but she should have known Damon would be there. The smart thing would have been to turn around and leave after she saw him, especially after the hurtful things he'd said that afternoon. How dare he imply that she invited unwanted male attention because of the way she dressed? What kind of chauvinistic bull crap was that? *Oh, why did he have to be so awful?*

But then ... that kiss ...

She'd never believed in such things as earth-shattering or soul-shaking, but nothing else came close to describing it. It was like her world had turned upside down. One moment, she was enraged at Damon and telling him off, and the next, they had had their mouths and hands all over each other. The feeling was nothing like she'd felt before, and even now, thinking about it got her hot and bothered.

But then he'd acted like a jerk again. No, he wasn't even close to jerk-like. He'd acted like a *monster*.

*Damn you.*

*Ruin my life.*

*Get out.*

*Go.*

Did he hate her that much? The thought of it made her chest ache something fierce. Tears sprang in her eyes, but she quickly wiped them away. If it wasn't apparent before, Damon obviously despised her. He probably kissed her to scare her away.

It should have worked too. Except her stupid, hussy of a body wanted *more*.

*I'm hopeless.*

Flopping onto her back, she gave up trying to sleep. Outside, the sky was turning pink. She slunk out of bed and headed to the bathroom. After finishing her business and washing her face, she reached for her sports bra, spandex top, and leggings hanging on the hooks behind the door. At least she had her gym clothes in her car when she left. Exercise would help her clear her thoughts. Endorphins were the one thing she could count on.

She tied her hair up in a ponytail, put on her running shoes, and then headed out of the bathroom, making a beeline for the front door.

"Hey, where're you going?"

"Jeez Louise!" Anna Victoria jumped back, clutching her hand to her chest. "J.D.? Are you okay?"

J.D. sat on the couch, still wearing last night's clothes, her arms stretched out over her head as she let out a deep yawn. "I'm great, thanks for asking."

"How are you feeling? Hungover?"

"Pshaw." She waved a hand dismissively. "Shifters don't get hangovers." Getting up from the couch, she raked her fingers through her disheveled blonde hair. "What happened to you last night?"

"I sent you a text," she said. "I wasn't feeling too well. Bourbon doesn't agree with me." After Damon had torn her blouse, there was no way she was going back in there. Besides, he told her to leave. So, she ran all the way to her car and drove home.

"I was so drunk, hon, I couldn't even see past my own face. So, where're you going?" J.D. nodded at her exercise clothes.

"Out for a jog," she said.

"Jog? This early?"

"I like to get my day started early. So, if you don't mind ..."

"Actually, I'd love to join you."

"Join me?"

J.D. blinked and rubbed her eyes. "Yeah. I haven't exercised in ... well, not ever. But, maybe I should, you know?"

"Er ... okay."

"Don't worry," J.D. said with a chuckle. "I'm a shifter. I can keep up. Besides, you're not familiar with the area, I don't want you getting lost. Give me five, and I'll meet you outside?"

"All right." Reaching for her coat, she put it on. "See you in five."

Soon, J.D. joined her outside. "Lennox Park is a couple of blocks away," she said. "There's a jogging trail around a man-made lake. It's really pretty any time of the year, even now in winter."

They walked a few blocks east until they reached the park and said jogging path. J.D. was right—it was beautiful out here, especially now just after dawn. The sun was already peeking from behind the mountains, bathing everything in a soft light. There were still patches of snow everywhere, which added to the winter wonderland feel of the place. She could almost forget about her problems and about last night, but it seemed like thoughts of Damon kept creeping into her mind. And when she did start thinking about him, she pushed herself harder.

Albuquerque never got this cold, but running definitely helped get her warm. After completing the jogging trail, she was sweating underneath her coat, so she unbuttoned it to let some cool air in.

"Woo, girl, you must be in good shape," J.D. remarked. "You're only winded now."

"Thanks," she replied. "It must be nice to have that shifter physique." J.D. wasn't even sweating, plus she was only dressed in a T-shirt and shorts.

"Yeah, it has its perks," she said. "But we're not all the same. And I'm not so flexible, plus I know I could be in better shape, like you. I mean, wow, how much do you work out?"

Anna Victoria laughed. "Exercise is kind of my thing." If there was one thing she was proud of, it was her physique. She didn't have the body of a weightlifter or anything, but she was in tip-top shape. "I got my B.A. in physical education from NMU. I thought it was an easy degree and would be mostly blow-off classes. But my teachers were pretty tough, and I found I liked it."

"Really? What other things did they teach you?"

"Well, I'm actually certified to teach Pilates and yoga," she said. "Though I've never really held a job in my field."

"Sounds like now is the time to put that degree to use."

"What do you mean?"

"I'll be your first ever yoga student. I know the perfect place too." J.D. dragged her across the park, toward a frozen lake. They walked across a wooden bridge where there was a gazebo in the middle of the water.

"Oh, this place is nice." The gazebo was covered in glass on all sides, and it was warm inside.

"C'mon, yoga teacher," J.D. said. "Teach me, I'm eager to learn."

She chuckled. "All right, but don't say I didn't warn you."

The two of them stood side by side as Anna Victoria led the flow. J.D. did well for her first time, though she wasn't flexible enough to do some of the more advanced poses.

"Rubber limbs aren't part of the shifter package," J.D. said with a laugh.

"You're pretty good, though. It's like you have the balance of a cat."

J.D. grimaced, and Anna Victoria suspected it wasn't just because they were in a One-Legged King Pigeon Pose. "Maybe you can show me how to put my leg behind my head. I bet that would make me popular with the boys."

Anna Victoria guffawed. "Maybe."

When she declared the session over, J.D. collapsed on the floor. "Whew. That was a real challenge. Thanks. Have you ever thought of doing this for real?'

"For real?"

"I mean, as a job. You could be an instructor."

"Huh." She'd never really thought about it. "Does Blackstone even have a yoga studio? Or a gym?"

"A gym wouldn't make money here," J.D. said. "Not with so many shifters."

"Yeah, everyone's pretty fit and hot around here. It's kind of distracting."

"Oh?" J.D. sat up, a sneaky smile on her face. "Is there a particular fit and hot guy that's caught your eye?"

"What? No!" She quickly turned around before J.D. could see her face burning. But the entire time, her brain—or maybe another organ—was screaming, *Damon.*

"Did you really go home by yourself last night?" J.D. teased. "Don't think I didn't notice that Damon went after you, and then you both disappeared from the party."

"Wait, what? He didn't go back?" She thought he had told her to leave because he didn't want her there.

"So, you *were* with him!" J.D. said, excited. "Tell me what happened!"

"I—" Though she tried to scamper away, J.D. reached out and grabbed her hands to prevent her from escaping. "It was ... meant nothing okay?" Oh, how was she going to get out of this?

"What meant nothing?" J.D. squeaked.

"Er ..." It was too late. And J.D. practically had her in a death grip. "We, uh, kissed and—"

"Holy. Freakin. Shit!" J.D.'s eyeballs looked like they were going to pop out of her face. "You and Damon kissed! I knew it!" She hopped to her feet excitedly. "I knew it!"

"Knew ... it?"

"When Gabriel told me who you were, and Damon acted weird around you ..." Her mouth clamped shut. "I mean ..." She cleared her throat. "Let's just say Damon hasn't, uh, dated much in the last couple of years. Not since he came home from the Special Forces."

"Special Forces?" Damon had been in the Army? Well ... that did make sense, with the way he was so organized and didn't waste time with pleasantries.

"Yeah." J.D. sat back down in front of her. "It was ... it's not my story to tell, but let's just say, when he came back from deployment... it was like he was a new person. Stuff happens over there, you know, things that we could only imagine. And since then ... it's like nothing makes him happy. Or sad. Or even excited. It's like he's come back as a shell of himself. Gabriel and I tried everything, but nothing worked. He's better now, at least, we can drag him out once in a while, but for the most part, he prefers to be alone."

Her chest tightened at the thought of Damon being lonely, as well as what could have happened to him while he was deployed. While she knew nothing about the military, if he had to leave, it was probably serious. "I didn't realize."

"He'd never show it or say anything. That's just the way he is. But ... you ... it's the first time he's shown any emotion toward anyone or anything."

She frowned. "Yeah, well, I wish he would show his hate toward someone else." Her shoulders slumped.

"Hate? What makes you say he hates you?"

"I ..." His words came back to her mind, but she couldn't say it out loud without her throat closing up. "Just ... trust me, he's not interested in me."

"But he kissed you!"

"Please don't tell anyone." She buried her face in her hands. "Maybe ... maybe I should quit now. I'm sorry, J.D. I can leave by Monday. I'll find a way to pay you back—"

"No way. Look at me, Anna Victoria." There was a fierce determination in her amber eyes. "You're not going to quit. You are not leaving Blackstone."

"But—"

"At first, I kind of thought you were one of those snotty girls who would laugh at me because I was such a tomboy, that I was nothing but a grease monkey's daughter. But no, you showed me how genuinely nice you were. And I know you love Blackstone already, and you want to live here."

J.D. was right of course; the more time she spent here, the more she wanted to stay.

"So, why don't you finish your two weeks? You just have five days to go right? Hmm ..." She scratched at her chin. "I have an idea."

"Idea? What?"

"I'm not one hundred percent sure yet, so you'll have to give me time. Give me until the end of the week. I might be able to line up another opportunity for you, but I have to check on a couple of things. Then you can tell me if you still want to stay here, okay?"

"I ... why would you do this for me, J.D.? I'm no one to you."

"I don't know, girl, but ... let's just say I have a feeling about you."

She stared back at J.D., flabbergasted. Gabriel had said the same words to her when they met. "I ... suppose I could wait another week." Going back to the station would be torture, but she would do her best to get through it.

"Great!" J.D. hopped to her feet and helped her up. "Now, I think we deserve a couple of slices of pie after this workout, what do you think?"

Anna Victoria laughed. "I think so too."

# Chapter 7

Since that disastrous night, Damon did all he could to avoid seeing Anna Victoria. Taking Matthew Lennox's advice, he put himself on the schedule for patrols. He also arrived at the station early in the morning before anyone else on the day shift did and left late in the evening to finish off his paperwork and other administrative work.

One good thing about this was being outside did him and his bear good. After last week's disaster, he realized that maybe he was also being too hard on his animal. It needed to get out too, and keeping it cooped up for too long would lead to more uncontrollable shifts, like what happened last week at The Den. He couldn't believe how he nearly ... almost ... shifted in front of her. *Not again.* What happened that night was evidence enough he should stay away and forget about her.

However, despite all his efforts, he couldn't completely eradicate Anna Victoria from his thoughts. It was like she lingered everywhere, especially around the office. He could smell traces of her sweet scent when he passed by her empty desk after she left for the day. The paperwork she left on his desk had handwritten sticky notes telling him what needed to be signed, but all he could do was stare at her loopy, feminine handwriting.

And of course, the memory of her taste was burned into his brain. Every spare thought he had was of her. And he was getting damned tired of it, so he did everything he could to distract himself, working himself till he was so exhausted, he couldn't think straight.

Even now, it was Saturday and his day off, he was still working. Though this particular task wasn't strictly on the schedule, it still had to be done, and it was a good excuse to get deeper into the mountains and away from anything and everything that reminded him of her.

The cabin in the distance came into view as Damon trudged through the snow. It had been an old, abandoned ranger station that had been retrofitted to become livable again. Currently, it only had one occupant, who was sitting on the porch steps. Of course, said occupant already knew someone was approaching.

"Hello, Damon," Milos Vasilakis greeted, his voice low and deeply accented.

"Hello, Milos."

"Long time no see." He got up and stretched out to full height. "I thought maybe you don't have time for visit, now that you are big-time chief, huh?"

He chuckled. "Yeah, they keep me busy. But I'm here now. How are you?"

Milos peered at him with his one good green eye. The other eye was missing and covered in scar tissue. "I'm well as can be. Would you like to come in and have a coffee?"

"Sure." He followed Milos into the cabin. It was large and clean and had all the basics. He noticed the half-empty pizza box on the kitchen table. "Was Petros just here?"

"Yes." Milos went to the counter and poured out coffee into two mugs. "But he had to leave because he was bringing his mate and child to some Winter Carnival."

*Right.* That was tonight. "Why didn't you join him?"

He shrugged as he put the mug on the table. "Would you go to such a thing?"

Damon winced. He supposed he deserved that; though he had never shared what happened to him with Milos, it was obvious that his wolf had sensed the same thing from Damon's bear—a brokenness that ran deep.

Milos had come to Blackstone about a year ago to seek revenge on his former friend and packmate, Petros Thalassa, a recent transplant to town from Greece who had mated with a local female wolf. Damon didn't have the details, but Milos had blamed Petros because he'd been captured by a nefarious anti-shifter organization who had tortured and performed experiments on him. Although he'd been caught and subdued, Petros had begged Matthew Lennox to spare Milos and that instead of sending him to shifter prison or back to their former pack, allow him to stay in Blackstone and get help. The Blackstone Dragon allowed him to stay deep in the mountains, as long as he didn't harm anyone.

Damon didn't know if Milos had pieced his life back together, even with his friend's help, but he had seen improvements over the last year. The wolf shifter had been quiet and sullen when he first came here, but after some time, he began to talk. Part of Damon's job in the rangers before he became chief was to bring Milos supplies, and they would always make small talk while having coffee.

"How is everything?" Damon asked as he took a sip of the coffee. "Were you okay during the blizzard?"

"Yes, do not worry about me. I may be from the islands, but

the snow did not bother me." Milos frowned. "Our *friend*, though ..." He looked outside the window, deep into the thick line of trees. "I have not heard from him in a while."

Guilt poured through him at the reminder that there was *one* other person living in these parts, even more isolated than Milos. "Is Krieger ... all right?"

"Maybe you should check for yourself. I have not seen him since before the blizzard."

Damon knew he should go. He owed it to Krieger. Things had been busy the past six months that he hadn't even had the time to see his former squad mate since his promotion.

At least, that's what he told himself. It was easier to ignore the guilt. As much as the incident had messed him up, it had nearly destroyed Krieger. And it had all been Damon's fault.

"Maybe I should." But some other time, when he wasn't in a tizzy up like this. Krieger tended to be sensitive about the moods of people, which was why he lived all the way up here. He abhorred company even more than Damon or Milos, though he and the wolf shifter seemed to get along well enough. Again, he knew it was because broken animals could sense each other.

They talked for a few more minutes before Damon said goodbye, and promised to have more supplies sent over the next week, including Milos's favorite donuts from the local bakery.

The trudge back to HQ took another hour, and it was already so late, that he expected the station to be nearly empty. So the sight of Gabriel, waiting for him by the door, took him completely by surprise. They hadn't spoken since their blowup, and they had mostly avoided each other during the party. Perhaps it was a good thing, since now Damon realized he had been acting like an asshole.

"Hey," Gabriel greeted.

"Hey." He paused, choosing his words carefully. "Why are you up here on a Saturday night?"

"Why are you?" Gabriel asked. "Even you don't work on weekends."

"I had a lot of stuff to do, plus I wanted to go see Milos."

"Oh. Is he all right?"

He nodded.

"And Krieger?"

"I didn't get the chance to check on him." Another awkward silence stretched between them, so he decided to just take the bull by the horns. "Gabriel, you were right. About last week."

"I was?"

"Yeah. About Anna Victoria. Last Friday, what I said to her was personal, and I should never have said them. And what I said to you, too, that was way out of line."

A myriad of emotions passed over the lion shifter's face. "I don't want her in that way. Anna Victoria is a sweet girl, and all J.D. and I wanted to do was help out someone in need. But," he scratched his chin, "what is it about her that's got you all up in knots? Do you really despise her that much? What did she do to you?"

Damon considered his options. He could lie to his friend, but the thought turned his stomach sour. He and Gabriel had always been open with each other, and there was no one he trusted more. So, he decided on the truth. "Anna Victoria is my mate."

"Excuse me?" Gabriel's jaw dropped down, then closed again. "Your mate? As in, your *mate*, mate?"

He nodded.

Gabriel looked truly shocked. "I mean, from the beginning with the way you acted around her ... I thought maybe you finally found someone who caught your eye, but I never thought you guys would be mates."

"Don't lions believe in mates?"

"It's uh, a little more complicated with prides." He rolled his shoulders back and rubbed the back of his head with his palm. "In my pride, anyway. We marry based on wealth and status. And who our Alpha chooses."

Damon had heard that certain types of shifters and groups had arranged marriages, but never really thought to ask Gabriel about the Russel Pride. "Oh. Do you already have a—"

"No," he said quickly. "But ... someday, Genevieve will probably find me a suitable lioness to marry. Anyway, let's not talk about me. So ... Anna Victoria, huh?" He chuckled and clapped him on the shoulder. "Congrats, man. I heard mating was a special thing."

"Don't congratulate me," he said. "I'm not planning to bond with her. Or even tell her."

"What?" Gabriel's voice rose a few decibels. "Not bond with her? Why the hell not?"

"You *know* why." Gabriel knew the whole story. And had been there for the aftermath. "I can't ... not with anyone."

"But she's your mate. Surely it wouldn't happen again. Not with her."

"I can't risk it." His hands tightened into fists.

"That was a long time ago," Gabriel pointed out. "It has to be better by now, right? Your animal—"

"Is exactly the same." He scrubbed a hand down his face. "Nothing's changed."

"But you said you were better."

"I am ... except for that." How could he even begin to explain to Gabriel what it was like? "I can't go through it again, and not with her. I wouldn't be able to forgive myself if I hurt her."

"But—"

"If there was even a chance I could harm her, I don't want to take it. Would you?"

"I wouldn't just leave her, not without giving it a chance." Gabriel scratched at his head. "For God's sake, this is a once-in-a-lifetime chance. You don't get another mate."

"She's human, she'll get over it. Hell, she doesn't even know. She still has a chance to find a husband and have kids." The Demon did not like that one bit and clawed at him, making him grit his teeth in pain.

"But—"

"But what about you?" Damon really didn't want to fight with Gabriel again, but he was pushing again. "If you found your mate but she wasn't a lioness your eldest sister picked? Would you give up everything for her?"

Gabriel's jaw hardened. "That's different."

"How?"

"For one thing, you deserve happiness after everything you've gone through."

Now *that* stunned him into silence.

"You don't want to bond with her?" Gabriel said. "Fine. Stay away then, and stop hurting her because you can't see what's right in front of you." He crossed his arms over his chest. "If you change your mind, I'm going to the Winter Carnival with J.D. and Anna Victoria. And maybe, just maybe, she'll find someone else who'll take care of her and cherish her the way she deserves." With that, he turned around and stomped off.

*Goddamn my fucking life!*

It was hard to breathe, hard to think. The Demon was furious at him, but it wasn't trying to take over. No, it wanted him to go to her, and claim her and bond with her.

But he couldn't do it. Not after what happened the last time.

The Demon roared at him in denial and shook its block head, as if saying, *no, we won't harm her. I promise.*

His heart slammed into his rib cage. The Demon had never done that before. Never promised him anything. Violence was its usual form of communication and bargaining. It never wanted anything as much as it wanted Anna Victoria, and it was as if it finally understood what had to be done.

But, could he risk it?

## Chapter 8

"Wow," Anna Victoria exclaimed as she looked at the sights around her. "This is amazing. I'm so glad you brought me here."

"It's only the second year they've done it," J.D. said. "But it was such a big success the first time, I guess the businesses decided to bring it back. It's a great way to get people to go out and spend after the holidays."

The Blackstone Winter Carnival was in full swing, and Main Street was dressed to the nines. The road was closed to vehicles, and various booths lined the street, selling everything from handcrafted winter wear to homemade baked goods and hot drinks. It was crowded, and everyone was in good spirits. Couples walked by holding hands, families flitted from booth to booth excitedly. As if on cue, snow began to flitter down from the sky.

"It's so magical." Anna Victoria closed her eyes, taking in the clean scent of the cold air.

"There's no snow where you come from?" J.D. asked.

"We do get snow," she explained. "Albuquerque's actually a

desert in high elevation, but around this time, we'll get one to two inches the whole month. Less than ten the entire season."

J.D. guffawed. "The whole month? You should have been here two weeks ago! We saw a record snowfall. Over thirty inches high up in the mountains, I think."

"Wow."

"C'mon." J.D. dragged her toward one of the booths. "I want to try this hot chocolate wine."

"Ooh, I'm in!" Thank goodness her paycheck finally came through yesterday. It was a relief, finally having some money to spare. It wasn't much, but she was able to set aside half of her rent, plus, she could afford to splurge on a few treats tonight. They lined up at the booth, chatting as they waited their turn.

"Hey, J.D.! Nice to see you here."

"Kate, you made it out! Glad to see you, too." J.D. greeted the woman who had come up to them. "Is that Sofia?" She nodded at the dark-haired child bundled up in winter gear at her hip. "She's so big."

"Yeah, she's getting big, my girl." She kissed the baby on the cheek, making her laugh. Sofia grabbed a handful of her mother's dark blonde locks which were tipped with aqua green and matched the studded jewel on her nose.

"By the way, Kate, this is Anna Victoria."

"Oh, so you're Anna Victoria. J.D.'s told me all about you." She held out her free hand. "Kate Caldwell-Thalassa. It's a mouthful, I know, but I didn't want to totally get rid of my maiden name. My husband's kind of traditional, so we compromised." Her eyes sparkled with mirth. "And this is my daughter, Sofia." The adorable baby giggled when Kate bounced her up and down.

"Hello, Sofia. And nice to meet you, too, Kate." She looked slyly at J.D. "What did J.D. tell you about me?"

"All good stuff," she said. "Actually, I'm glad we bumped

into each other. If you guys don't have anywhere to be, we should go have a chat with the others."

"Others?" Anna Victoria asked.

"Yeah, we can come with you." J.D. winked at her. "Trust me."

With a shrug, she followed J.D. and Kate toward the parking lot behind the diner. Half of the space had been converted to a dining area with picnic tables scattered around. They headed over to one of the tables where a couple of women were sitting down, chatting and laughing as they sipped their drinks.

"Look who I found!" Kate exclaimed.

"Hey, guys," J.D. greeted. "Oomph, it's been a while. All your kids are growing like weeds!"

Two of the women held children in their laps. One of them was a pretty blonde woman who was wrangling a rambunctious older boy. "Tell me about it. I can't keep my eye off Devon for a second or else." She grimaced, then looked up at Anna Victoria. "Hello there, have we met?"

"Oh, sorry!" J.D. said. "Girls, this is Anna Victoria. Anna Victoria, these are the girls," she announced with a chuckle.

"Hi, everyone," she greeted.

"That's Catherine, Devon's mama," J.D. began. "You've met Catherine's husband, Matthew."

"It's lovely to meet you, Mrs. Lennox," she said.

"Please, it's Catherine," she said. Her accent was posh and refined. "So, you're Anna Victoria. You were at the ranger station, right? I've heard about you from Matthew."

"I owe your husband a lot. I'm sure he's told you how he helped me get my job."

J.D. continued. "And beside her is Christina," she nodded to the other blonde.

"You're twins." Her gaze ping-ponged between them.

Christina laughed. "At least our husbands aren't here, though I still can't believe people think they're twins." Catherine nodded in agreement.

"Christina is married to Jason Lennox, Matthew's twin brother," Kate explained.

Anna Victoria was introduced to the two remaining women —a pretty, petite brunette named Georgina Lennox who was also married to a Lennox brother, and Amelia Grimes, who held a sleeping, angel-faced baby boy named James.

"Where's Dutchy?" J.D. asked, glancing around.

"You know, I haven't seen her around." Christina tapped at her chin. "But I'm sure she's busy with work. Anyway," she scooted over and motioned for Anna Victoria to join her while J.D. sat next to Georgina. "J.D. tells me you're a fitness instructor."

Her head whipped toward J.D. "You told them that?"

"You got your B.A. and all the certifications. And you led me through that awesome yoga workout. You're an instructor, hon." J.D. proclaimed. "This is the idea I was telling you about at the park last week. I talked to the girls," she gestured at the women at the table, who all nodded along, "and we want you to start yoga, Pilates, and fitness classes. We'll be your first clients, and eventually you can open up classes to other people in Blackstone."

"But Blackstone's a shifter town," she protested. "Everyone here's super fit. Would anyone even want to take classes with me?"

"I'm not a shifter," Georgina said. "And neither are Catherine and Christina."

"I could use some exercise," Catherine said. "Soon I'll be running after a dragonling who can fly." She nodded at Devon, who was now trying to grab at all the glasses on the table.

"And I haven't been to yoga in forever," Christina added.

"My job's demanding, and the nearest studio is all the way in Verona Mills. I don't have time to drive there and back."

"Even though I'm a shifter, my neck and back still ache after a couple of hours at the drafting table," Amelia said. "A yoga workout could help me out."

"But where would we have it?" Anna Victoria bit her lip. "I don't have a place."

"We can do it at the castle," Catherine said. "It'll be great."

"The castle?" Anna Victoria asked. "There's a castle here?"

Catherine chuckled. "Yeah, Blackstone Castle. There should be enough space in the ballroom and it has a gorgeous view of the mountains. Just tell me what you need. Mats or towels or whatever, and I'm sure I can find some in storage somewhere."

"It'll be great," J.D. assured her. "Imagine, charge each one of us a reasonable amount for the class, you can earn some good money."

Anna Victoria was speechless. If she could get a couple of people to pay a minimum amount that could be enough to earn some extra cash. And then maybe eventually she could quit the job at the ranger station. "Th-thank you guys. I've only ever taught during my certification exams, but I won't let you down."

Everyone seemed happy and encouraging, and she asked them about what else they wanted to learn and their expectations. She felt giddy at the thought that she was actually going to do something she was good at and get paid for it.

"I'm starving. I'm going to go and get some food," she declared a while later. "I might head over to the pretzel stand. Can I get you guys something?"

When no one asked for anything, she got up and headed back toward Main Street. *Hmmm, where was that pretzel stand?* They had only briefly passed by it, but she remembered it might have been in front of the hardware store.

Turning back toward Main Street, she saw that it was even more crowded than it had been earlier. So, she decided to take a shortcut behind the book store and loop around.

She clutched her coat tighter as she darted between two buildings. There were no street lamps to illuminate the empty lot, but there was enough reflected light from Main Street that she wasn't completely blind. Even so, there was an eerie quality about being alone out here.

A shiver ran down her spine. *What the—*

Her heart hammered in her chest as goosebumps rose on her arms. Swallowing hard, she glanced around. It was like there were eyes on her, watching her, but there was no one else here. But for some reason, her instincts were telling her to *run*.

Spinning on her heel, she made a mad dash toward Main Street. But something solid blocked her way and a pair of hands grabbed at her arms.

She screamed. "Get away from me!" Panic tightened her chest, and her muscles locked up. Oh God, she'd been too complacent. Let her guard down because Blackstone felt like a sleepy little town where nothing happened. And now she was in danger. Tears prickled at her eyes.

"Stop. Stop! Anna Victoria, it's me."

*That voice ...*

A dizzy spell threatened to overwhelm her and her knees went weak.

"Breathe. C'mon, sweetheart, breathe for me."

And she did. Opened her mouth and took in a big gulp. And then another. And one more until she felt somewhat normal again. "I ... Damon?" Was she hallucinating? No, she wasn't. It really was *him*. Joy and relief sparked in her chest as the tightness ebbed away. "What are you doing here?"

"Are you all right?" His mouth pulled back in a tight line.

"You're shaking. Are you crying? What's the matter? What scared you?"

"It's ... it's nothing. I—" *Oh.* His arms wound around her and pulled her to his chest. Damon's body heat permeated through her coat and her clothes, and an odd, calming sensation ran through her. Memories of last week's kiss came rushing back in her mind, but she didn't mind. Not when she felt safe.

"I saw you running; you looked like you'd seen a ghost," he murmured into her hair. "What happened?"

"I'm fine ... just scared myself, walking in dark parking lots. Uh, Damon?"

"Hmm?"

"Er, do you mind?" She wiggled around. "I can't breathe." His grip had tightened and her nose was pressed against his chest.

He quickly let go of her. "Oh. Right. Sorry."

An awkward pause stretched between them. "What are you doing here? I mean—you know, what? Never mind." She rubbed her arms. "It's a public event. Of course you're here." What did she mean by asking him that, anyway? Everyone was here after all, but she didn't really expect to run into him.

"Anna Victoria—"

"It's okay." Her hands went up defensively. "We don't have to do this, not when we're in public and both obviously on our personal time. I know I'm such a nuisance, and you don't want me around so—"

"You're not. And ... and I don't."

She frowned. "Don't what?"

"You're not a nuisance. And I want you around."

She huffed. "You certainly have a funny way of showing it. Listen, you don't have to pretend. A-and maybe I'll be out of your hair soon. End of the month. Next month, tops."

His body went all stiff. "What do you mean?"

"I found something else," she said. "Not right away, but I'll be fine. I mean, it's already been two weeks, and I got my paycheck and HR didn't say anything about renewing, so I figured you didn't want me—"

"It's not that. I—" He took a step toward her and then paused. "I want you, Anna Victoria."

"I told you, you don't have to pretend—"

"I said, I *want* you." His tone had a low, gravelly quality that made a delicious shiver run down her spine. "I've wanted you the first moment I saw you. I can't stop thinking about that kiss."

Her jaw dropped open. "But you ... you walked away."

"I know."

"And you said ... you said I ruined your life. You told me to go away."

He took in a sharp breath. "No! I mean, it wasn't you I was talking to."

"Huh? It was just you and me there."

"Yes but ..." He raked his fingers through his hair. "I was ... I was talking to my animal. My bear."

"Your ... bear?"

"I don't know where to begin. But know this, Anna Victoria. I want you. Don't ever think I don't." He looked her straight on, his green eyes ablaze. "How can I not? You're my mate, and I won't ever want anyone else but you."

"I'm your *what*?"

"Er, I wasn't going to lead with that, but ..." He rubbed the back of his head. "You don't know much about shifters, do you?"

She shook her head. "Almost nothing."

"We ... our animals recognize their mates right away. When I saw you at The Den, it immediately told me. You're mine. My mate."

"Like ... soul mates?" Was he serious?

"Something like that. No one can really explain it ... it just is. You just know. "

"But I'm not a shifter."

"It doesn't matter. Lots of shifters have human mates. But I don't know what it's like for you. You probably don't feel the pull as much as I do, since you don't have an animal inside you that tells you."

Her knees felt weak, and she was lightheaded again. *Mates?* How was it possible? "Surely there's a mistake."

"No, there's no mistake. You're the one."

The expression on his face told her he was dead serious. "But you ... you've been avoiding me. Acting like a jerk around me."

He looked at her sheepishly. "And I'm sorry. It hurt me more to do that, but I was fighting it. I didn't want to hurt you."

"H-hurt me?"

He took a long, deep breath. "My animal ... it's not normal. I'm ... it's ... I call it The Demon. Because it's out of control. And I've ... hurt someone before."

Fear made her take a step back. She should run away, right now. But there was a part of her that wanted to know everything. "Tell me. Tell me what happened."

"I ..." His face turned blank, and there was a hollow look in his eyes. "My last mission. Kargan, the largest city in Durusha, an independent nation between the border of Turkmenistan and Afghanistan. We were supposed to be a peacekeeping force, made up of shifter and human soldiers. I was the commanding officer. It was Sunday. Market day." He swallowed hard. "Intelligence initially said it was safe to go inside the market building. I sent a small team to investigate a secret cell of a well-known terrorist group.

"But at the last minute, my instinct said something was wrong. So I ran after them. I didn't make it. The explosion ...

it leveled the entire building. It was chaos ... people running in the opposite direction as I tried to get to my team. There were too many, and they were trampling me. I was getting hurt, so ... my bear took over. I don't remember much, but I've seen some footage. It wasn't pretty." He grimaced. "It took three rounds of tranquilizers to stop me. And when I woke up, I was told my entire team perished. At least we thought so. One member survived. He'd been trapped in the building for three days."

*It's like he's come back as a shell of himself.* J.D.'s words made so much sense now. "Oh, Damon." She didn't know why, but she took a step forward and placed a hand on his cheek. "It wasn't your fault. It was the terrorists who blew up that building."

"I was the commanding officer." His jaw remained set, but he turned his face to nuzzle at her palm, a move that made electricity shoot up her arm. Then he froze and pulled her hand away. "They put me on leave, and I went to all the shrinks and doctors they told me to go to. I wanted to be well. And to get back into action. After six months, I thought I was getting better. Hated crowds, still do, but I was getting better. Until ..." He took a deep breath. "Only Gabriel knows about this. It was covered up. But ... if you want to stay away from me after you hear this, I'll understand."

"What happened?" She was itching to know. "Please, just tell me."

"I don't want to, because I don't want you to know what a monster I truly am, but I will because you deserve the truth." Soulful green eyes bore into her. "I was out with my buddies, these guys I went to boot camp with. We were at a bar outside Fort Carson and these base bunnies, er, girls were there. They were ... friendly."

She grimaced, which made him wince. Clearing her throat

—and trying to ignore that ugly, jealousy rising up in her—she said, "Go on."

"I went home with one of them. So, we're at her place. On her couch. And I ... The Demon starts going crazy. That's not something normal. See, it's taboo for animals to make their presence known when, uh, their human sides are getting intimate."

"It's not?"

"It's just not done; it's their instinct to leave shit like that alone. They don't get involved in our sexual lives. But my bear ... it wouldn't stay away. I tried ignoring it, but when I did, it only got louder and more violent. I ... shifted again without meaning to. I lost control, blacked out. When I woke up ... I was in the base hospital."

"A-and the woman?"

"She got scared and ran away, but Command had her tracked down. The general at the time did all he could, used every resource, to make sure she didn't say anything about what happened. Shifters like me—the ones in the military—we're too valuable. They didn't want a scandal, so they covered everything up. But I was discharged after that." He buried his face in his hands. "I can't ... that's why I can't claim you as my mate ... I could hurt you. I nearly did that night we kissed."

"But you *didn't* hurt her, and you didn't hurt me," she pointed out. "And as for your guys ... that's not your fault. Like you said, you got bad intelligence and you tried to help them."

"It doesn't change the fact that five good men died, and I ruined the life of a good friend," he said. "I was their commanding officer."

God, the hurt in his eyes was too much. Her throat was burning with tears for him. "I'm so sorry, Damon. I had no idea ... thank you for telling me all this. It can't be easy."

"You deserve to know the truth. It doesn't excuse the way

I've been treating you. I promise to be better. But now you know why I can't ... why we can't be together. I can't risk it. I can't risk you."

The finality of his words plucked at her chest, making it ache fiercely. She had only known they were mates five minutes ago, and yet something inside her screamed that this wasn't right. Her mouth opened, but nothing came out.

"I'll find a way for you to keep the job, while avoiding each other. I've done it this week, so I can keep out of your way until you've found something else."

She watched him turn on his heel and walk away from her. Again, there it was. In her mind. In her heart. Her entire being saying, *no, this was wrong*. She'd never felt like this, perhaps because for the first time in her life, there was finally something in her life worth fighting for.

"Damon!" she called as she sprinted after him. "Stop! Please."

He turned around. "What—*mmm!*"

Her body propelled into him, and he caught her just in time as she leapt up to kiss him. *Oh my*. Her arms snaked around his neck; her mouth desperate as she pressed her lips against his. He didn't respond, at least not for the first two seconds. But soon, his mouth moved under hers. Hands lifted her up, and she had no choice but to wrap her legs around his waist.

He let out a soft growl, nipped at her lips, then devoured her mouth. The kiss deepened, his tongue slipping between her teeth to coax hers out. God, he tasted like the warm sun and grass and nature, and every delicious masculine thing she could think of. Everything about this moment, the way their mouths melded, their tongues danced, bodies pressed against each other, the heat surrounding them, was just *perfect*. She didn't want it to end, but he pulled away.

Leaning his forehead against hers, he let out a sigh. "I'm too broken for you," he said. "We shouldn't do this. I'm a mons—"

"Stop saying that." True anger bubbled in her. "And so that's it?" She slid out of his grasp but didn't back away. Instead she stood toe-to-toe with him. "You get to decide all this? What about what I want?"

"And what do you want?"

"I ..." She took his hands in hers. "I want you, too, Damon. I'm not a shifter, I don't have an animal inside me, but I do know I want you. I can feel it in my soul, you and me. This is how it's supposed to be."

"But I could hurt you."

"You can't." Gripping his hands tighter, she pulled them to her lips and kissed his fingers. "I'm your mate, right? Why would your bear hurt me?"

He stiffened. "What do we do now?"

What indeed? "Why don't you ... walk me back to the diner? We don't have to go out there," she cocked her head toward the crowded Main Street, "but maybe we can just talk."

"All right." He took one of her hands and threaded it through his. "Lead the way."

They walked hand in hand, through empty parking lots, making their way back to the diner.

"Anna Victoria ... will you have dinner with me? Next week?" he asked.

Her heart fluttered in her chest. "Yes," she agreed. "That would be nice."

"There's an Italian restaurant in town, or we could check out one of the newer places in South Blackstone," he said.

"Will you be okay going out?" she asked, squeezing his hand.

"A restaurant on a weeknight should be fine," he said. "Just ... no clubs or crowded bars."

"Whatever you decide will be fine," she said. "Oh, here we are." They arrived at the lot behind the diner. J.D. and the other girls were still sitting at the table, though there were more people with them now. Gabriel was there, but she also recognized Matthew Lennox, and the man beside him was definitely his twin.

"Anna Victoria!" J.D. waved at them. "What happened? You were gone so long and ... Damon?" Her eyes practically popped out of their sockets when her gaze landed on their linked hands. "Guys?" She smirked at them. "Care to tell us what's going on?"

Her cheeks warmed as several pairs of eyes fixed on them.

"It's all right," Damon began. "Anna Victoria is my mate."

"You're shitting me, right? She's your mate?" J.D. exclaimed. "I had a feeling there was something special about her since you've never shown an interest in any female in forever, but I didn't think it was *that*."

"Congratulations, Damon," Matthew said. "A mate and the bond is a special thing." He looked at Catherine, his face completely lighting up.

Everyone offered their congratulations as well, including Gabriel. "Well, I'm glad it didn't take you another week to get your head outta your ass," he said, clapping him on the shoulder.

"Gabriel knew?" J.D. shot Damon a look of betrayal. "Before me?"

"I only found out about an hour ago," the lion shifter said defensively. "And that was after I cornered him back at the station. So," he turned to them. "What's next?"

"Next?" Damon's brows drew together.

"We're going on a date next week," Anna Victoria offered.

"I want it to be special," Damon admitted.

"Next week?" J.D. tsked and shook her head. "What the hell are you waiting for? Spring?" She slapped Damon on the shoulder, then gestured around them, "This is a winter carnival. It's snowing. They have hot drinks and sweet junk food you can feed each other while you canoodle. How much more special can you get?"

"Well, I—"

Gently, she turned them around and pushed them away from the picnic table. "Here. It's your first date. Now, go and be romantic, make out in public until everyone around you is sick, and," she winked at Anna Victoria, "don't do anything I wouldn't do. Which isn't a whole lot, by the way."

"J.D.," Damon warned.

She rolled her eyes. "You guys deserve this. I won't wait up." She wiggled her eyebrows at Anna Victoria. "Now *go*."

She looked up at him. "We don't have to do anything if you don't want to."

And then he surprised her, as a smile lit up his face. It was a true, genuine one and sent her heart aflutter once again. "I want to." He lifted her hand to his mouth and pressed a kiss on her palm. "There's nothing else I want more."

## Chapter 9

Damon couldn't recall the last time he'd enjoyed himself. Or had been this happy. And he knew, it was because of Anna Victoria.

It wasn't just because she was his mate, it was everything about her. The way her pansy-blue eyes sparkled when she laughed. Or how she gestured with her hands when she talked. Simply put, being around her made him happy.

The Demon, too, seemed content. In fact, except for a satisfied chuff here and there, it was mostly quiet, staying out of his way.

"Are you okay?" she asked, her face full of concern. "Is this too much? Do you want to move somewhere else?"

Since the crowds on Main Street were too much for him, they decided to go around the shops and stick to the less crowded backstreets. The library was located at the far end of Main Street and had fewer people, but they had kept the lights on so people could sit on the benches in front of the building. Anna Victoria had volunteered to get them food and drinks, insisting that he needed to stay and "save their prime spot" under one of the street lamps, but he knew it was her way of not making him feel bad about his anxiety in crowds.

"No, this is fine." He reached over and plucked free a snowflake stuck between her lashes. "But you must be freezing."

"Then keep me warm," she said saucily.

He put his cup of hot chocolate down. "Now, I like that idea." Snaking an arm around her shoulders, he pulled her close, leaning down to press his lips to hers. This was the first time he'd attempted to kiss her tonight since their last kiss in the parking lot behind the hardware store. It was just his luck that he'd parked one building over and saw her, looking frightened. He didn't know what spooked her, but he was glad he had caught up with her and they were able to iron things out. Telling her she was his mate hadn't been his plan, nor was baring his soul to her, but he couldn't stand the idea that she thought he didn't want her, not when the only thing he wanted was her.

She moaned against his mouth and moved closer to him, her lips warm and eager. Unable to stop himself, he hauled her onto his lap, their bodies urgently pressing against each other underneath all their layers of clothing.

"Anna Victoria," he began as he pulled away. "I know this is only our first date but—"

"Yes," she said, cutting him off.

He chuckled. "You don't even know what I'm going to ask you."

Unmistakable desire glittered in her eyes. "If you're asking me to go back to your place, then the answer is *definitely* yes."

Her words shot lust straight to his groin, and he groaned when his erect cock brushed up against her. "I ..."

"Well? What *were* you going to ask me?"

He couldn't recall now exactly. "Yes. I mean, I want you to come home with me."

"Good." She laid her head on his chest and took a deep breath. "I love your cabin. It's so beautiful out there."

"Mm-hmm." He inhaled her sweet scent as he nuzzled at her temple. "I'm glad." Pulling her up, he tucked her hand into his arm. "My truck's parked not too far away. Let's go."

They giggled and kissed like young lovers as they made their way to the parking lot. He opened the door for her and helped her inside, then rounded the vehicle back to the driver's side.

Her presence and scent filling the small cab of his truck was overwhelming, and it was a wonder he even managed to start the truck or even make the drive back without losing his patience and just taking her right there. He was nearly home when he remembered something important, something she may not have realized about his confession earlier.

Pulling in front of his cabin, he cut off the engine and turned to her. "There's something else you should know. And I don't know how you're going to react to this."

"What is it?" She blinked up at him. "I promise, I won't judge."

"Well ..." He rubbed his palm on the back of his head. "That woman ... back in Fort Carson. She was the last woman I tried to sleep with."

"Oh."

"That was six years ago."

Her lips rounded into a perfect circle. "*Oh.*"

"Yeah, and before that ... it was six months of therapy, and we'd been deployed for about four months so there wasn't much dating back there." God, it was embarrassing to admit this.

"So ... it's been over seven years for you."

He nodded. "I just ... I never felt a strong urge, not after what happened. Sure, I took care of myself, but other than that ..."

"It's nothing to be embarrassed about," she said. "I mean,

I'm sure you'll do fine." She patted his hand. "I can show you if you don't remember," she teased.

He burst out laughing. "I think I can figure out the basics."

She let out a yelp as he reached for her and hauled her onto his side of the cab, planting her on his lap. "I'm sure I can. There is something else ... I don't have protection on me. I should have gotten some before we drove up here, but I was just distracted. Shifters can't get STDs, so there was no reason for me to buy condoms—"

"Shh ..." Her finger landed on his lips. "It's all right. I'm safe. Up to date with my shots."

With a soft growl, he nipped at her forefinger. The thought of being in her without any barriers between them made his blood heat. But still ... "Are you sure—"

"Yes." Her pupils blew up with desire. "Please, Damon."

He opened the door, stepped out of the truck, and hauled her over his shoulder. She let out a yelp of surprise, but he couldn't help himself. Her giggles told him she was enjoying it too. "I've wanted to do that since ... well, since we met," he confessed when they got inside his cabin. He placed her on her feet, and she looked up at him with a skeptical expression.

"No you—"

He silenced her with his mouth. Now that they were inside his den, alone, an urgency set him off. He needed her so bad. Right. Fucking. *Now.*

She had already taken her coat off, so he did the same with his jacket. They continued kissing as they made their way up the stairs, their mouths only parting when necessary. Soon, they were in his bedroom, and she was only in her bra and panties, and he was in his boxers. Grabbing her by the waist, he hauled her to the bed, dropping her in the middle as he stood back.

"God, you're so fucking perfect."

Perfect skin everywhere. Her breasts were high and perky,

just the right size—he could probably cover them with both his hands. Small waist, flat stomach, with her hips rounding out to an ass that made him weep. Her legs were lean and long, strong too, as he recalled earlier when she wrapped them around him.

She swallowed and her nostrils flared as her gaze roamed over him. From the strong smell of her arousal, he knew she liked what she saw.

He stripped off his boxers, crawled over her, and moved between her legs, letting his cock brush against her. "I want you so bad, Anna Victoria."

Her hands came up to his shoulders, gripping them as she pushed her hips up at him. "Yes."

God, if he wasn't careful, he could embarrass himself right then and there. Gritting his teeth, he bent his head to kiss her slender neck as his hands moved down to her bra. Pulling the cups down, he cradled her soft breasts, his thumbs easily teasing her nipples to hardness. Moving lower still, he trailed kissed down between them, before taking a hardened bud into his mouth.

"Ah!" Her fingers dug into his scalp as her body arched toward him. He took the nipple deeper, sucking it in and teasing it with his tongue as he unsnapped her bra and tossed it aside. Trailing a hand down her body, he placed it on her stomach, pressing her down on the mattress. The way her hips were rubbing against his was too much. He wanted to last longer, savor her, and watch her come.

In one motion, he flipped her over so she was on top of him. Fuck, she was gorgeous, especially in the moonlight. Her breasts were thrust up, the small waist dipping into her hips. He reached between them where she was pressed down on his stomach, only a scrap of lace between them. Yanking the delicate fabric aside, he touched her slick lips, groaning inwardly at how ready she was.

"Damon," she panted as she rocked her hips against his fingers.

"That's it sweetheart," he urged, gently coaxing her onto her knees. He ripped her panties off, exposing the neat little triangle of dark blonde hair to his gaze and then slid a finger inside her. Fuck, she was so hot, rocking against his hand, fucking herself on his fingers. "Go on ... Come for me."

She moaned and moved her hips faster, harder. He slipped another finger inside her, going deeper, trying not to think about how tight she was as he might explode just thinking of being in there.

"Ngghhh!" Her body thrashed as she squeezed him tight, his fingers flooding with her juices. She collapsed on top of him, but he held her back.

"Not done yet, sweetheart."

Grabbing the cheeks of her ass, he hauled her up higher, until her legs straddled his head.

"Damon? What are you—oh!"

Bringing her down, he mouthed her slick, hot pussy. Dear God, she tasted sweet, like icing on a birthday cake with just a pinch of salt. He licked at her eagerly, exploring her, tickling her, teasing her until she was once again shaking with pleasure.

"I want to watch you on top," he said. "But I might not last too long."

She rolled over beside him. "Then you take charge," she said. "Take me, Damon."

With a soft growl, he covered her body with his. He grabbed at her wrists, pinning them over her head with one hand. She shivered, her mouth parting and her pupils dilating with arousal. Settling himself between her legs, he parted them, nudging at her entrance.

Sweat beaded on his temple as he pushed in, slowly. She let out a sharp cry, so he slowed down, allowing her to adjust to his size. When her body relaxed, he moved in again, his jaw in pain from gnashing his teeth together too hard.

She sighed when he stopped. "Are you all the way in?"

He shook his head.

"Dear God." She threw her head back. "What have I—oh!"

He pushed forward. "Now I'm in," he said, grinning at her. "Hold on, sweetheart."

"Oh my—oh!" She cried out when he suddenly pulled back and thrust back inside. Holding her tight, he moved in and out of her, enjoying the feel of her tightness squeezing with each pump. She was close to coming again, he could tell.

"Yes, oh God, yes!"

He moved faster, rutting into her as hard as he could. Her breath was coming in short, fast spurts, so he held her until she exploded, shaking all over as her hips undulated against his. He slowed his pace, easing her down until she was all limp.

"Not yet, sweetheart," he said, kissing her ear. "I need more."

Flipping her onto her stomach, he hauled her ass up and onto her knees, her elbows bracing her front on the bed. Bending down, he licked at her. "You taste so sweet. Like sugar." It was intoxicating; he could feast on her the whole day, but his cock was aching to be inside her again.

She gasped, then let out a cry when he thrust into her. He grabbed onto her hips, digging his fingers into the soft flesh as he fucked into her. His cock pistoned in and out, until she was making those sexy little pants that signaled her orgasm.

Pulling her up, he held her against his body, his front to her back, his cock going deeper inside her. His hand moved between her legs and plucked at her clit, sending her over the edge. He plowed into her; his control razor-thin. He wanted this feeling to last, but he'd been waiting for this forever. With a low, animalistic growl, he let go, coming deep inside her in the most intense orgasm he'd ever felt.

Her body went limp, and he let go for a moment so she could crash on the bed as he gathered his wits. Not that he had any left. His mind was completely and utterly shot. And he loved every second of it.

When he regained control of his body, he lay down next to her. He tried to grasp words, things he could say to her, but his mouth wouldn't cooperate.

Finally, she broke the silence. "I think you remembered more than the basics."

He burst out laughing, then cuddled her against him. "Are you ... good?"

"Better than good." She nuzzled against his chest. "And see, you didn't lose control. You didn't hurt me."

"I'll be damned." He was flabbergasted. Even now, there was only silence from his animal. Sure, he could feel its presence, like it was slumbering. But it didn't try to fight him or even interfere.

Her fingers traced circles on his pecs. "Maybe you just needed to get back in the saddle."

He snatched her hand and kissed her fingers. "Or maybe all I needed was you."

## Chapter 10

Anna Victoria couldn't remember if she'd ever woken up smiling in her life, but she definitely had one on her face this morning. Waking up came with full awareness of where she was and what happened last night—and it had her mentally fanning herself. *Woo.* Was there a word for hotter than hot? Like, surface of the sun hot? Because that's what it was like. The sheets would have probably burned up. Oh Lord, why did no one tell her shifters had an amazing recovery time? Damon didn't let her sleep for *hours*.

She stretched her arms over her head, aware of the delicious aches and pains all over her body. Damon's scent was all over the sheets, but as she reached over to the other side of the bed, she only grasped ... paper?

"Huh?" Sitting up, she rubbed her eyes and looked at the piece of paper in her hand. *Join me outside*, read the neat, masculine handwriting.

Another smile broke out on her face. She glanced out the large windows, which had an amazing view of the snow-covered trees. It was already light out, though in this weather, it was always hard to tell what time it was exactly. Still, it would be cold, which meant she needed to be prepared.

Climbing out of the massive bed, she grabbed the shirt hanging from the bed post—Damon's shirt which he had retrieved sometime last night—and put it on, then grabbed the blanket and padded out of the room, taking the stairs to the ground floor. Wrapping the blanket around her, she opened the door and braced herself for the cold. The chill hit her face, and she closed her eyes, breathing in the clean, crisp air. But where was Damon?

A growl made her eyes snap open. A small yelp escaped her mouth when she realized she wasn't alone. A large—no, *humungous*—dark brown bear was on the lawn, digging at the snowy ground.

She should have felt afraid. But her body didn't tense nor did her heart start racing. Instead, a calmness wrapped over her, and she instantly realized who it was. "Damon," she whispered.

The bear must have heard her, because its head swung over in her direction. Her breath caught in her throat as she recognized those green eyes. "Damon," she called again.

Though it hesitated at first, the bear eventually began to lumber toward her. Not minding the chill, she stepped out of the cabin and onto the porch, her steps almost mirroring Damon's animal. When she got to the bottom of the stairs, the bear was already there, bent down, waiting on all fours. Reaching out, she gently placed her hand on the bear's head.

"Oh, you're so soft." The fur was thick between her fingers. She ran her hand over the bridge of the bear's nose, and then up its head. The bear let out a satisfied chuff when she scratched at the crown.

Fascination made her grow bolder as she examined the bear closely. She'd never even see a live bear, much less petted one. *But it's not just any bear.* No, this was also Damon.

The bear pulled back, and she jumped in surprise. The air around her seemed to change and shift, and slowly, the animal's large frame began to shrink. Fur sank into skin, claws into hands. Seeing him transform ... it wasn't uncomfortable exactly, but it was like watching something private. Still, she couldn't turn away.

Finally, when it was all done, Damon was there, kneeling on one knee at the foot of the stairs. His head lifted, and his gaze met hers. "You're up."

"Yes," she said. "That was ..."

He frowned as he got to his feet. "I hope you weren't frightened. Or disgusted."

"What?" she exclaimed. "No, of course not. I was fascinated, but not disgusted." How could she be? This was a major part of him.

A smile—a rare, sincere one—lit up his face. "I'm glad." He hopped up the porch, grabbed the pajama bottoms hanging on the banister and put them on. Taking her hand, he led her to the outdoor couch on the other end of the wraparound porch and sat down.

"Come." He stretched out his arm, and moved over to make room for her.

Following his lead, she threw the blanket around them and cuddled up to him. "Hmm, so warm." She nuzzled at his chest. "You're like my own personal heater," she joked.

"Shifter metabolism." He pulled her tighter to him. "All good?"

She nodded. "You should have woken me up when you did."

"I would have, but I haven't slept yet."

Her head bobbed up to meet his gaze. "You haven't?"

"Nope." He tucked the other end of the blanket under her chin. "Don't need much rest. My bear was feeling restless, so I let him out. Plus, I'd rather watch you while you're sleeping." His lips brushed across hers. "You're so beautiful when you do."

"Oh, stop."

"You are." His voice took on that low, sensuous tone that made her melt.

She sighed and laid her head on his shoulder. It'd snowed heavily up here last night, and now everything was covered in a thick blanket of white, muffling the sounds and creating a calm, quiet feeling to their surroundings. "I can see why you'd want to live up here. It's so lovely and soothing."

"When I first came back from the army and I was a mess, coming up here was the only way I could escape." His fingers stroked her hair gently. "When I said that to Gabriel, he got this idea that I should join the Rangers. I was skeptical at first, but then he said he'd go through the training with me."

"He did?"

"Yeah. He hates this nature stuff, you know," he said.

"But it's been five years, and he's still working with you."

He chuckled. "Yeah. Now, he doesn't like to talk about it, but Gabriel doesn't need to work."

"He doesn't?"

"He's one of the majority shareholders of his family's company, Lyon Industries, and sits on the board of the Lucas Lennox Foundation. His trust fund could buy my house a hundred times over."

"Wait." She glanced up at him. "Gabriel is *rich*?"

"Not Lennox rich," he said. "But, yeah."

"Huh." She pondered on that. Now some things about the lion shifter did make sense. "He's a great friend then."

"He is." A wistful smile crossed his face. "Anyway, that's how I ended up with the Rangers. Also, I cashed out my army pension, my parents gave me some of the profits from the sale of their house, and then I got this place."

"It really is beautiful," she said, taking a deep whiff of the clean air.

"I'm glad you like it," he said.

"Really?"

He nodded. "Because I want you to spend more of your time up here with me ... if you want to, that is."

"I do want to," she said before thinking. There was a giddy feeling that rose up in her, but then she realized that everything seemed so sudden. "As long as you don't feel like I'm smothering you or this is all moving too fast." She knew guys could be sensitive when it came to women taking over their space. The last guy she had dated wouldn't even let her keep a toothbrush at his place.

A chuckle made his chest rumble. "Fast? Oh, sweetheart, these last two weeks have been torture. I told you, I wanted you from the beginning."

She worried at her lip and drew her brows together as she recalled his words last night, about being his mate. Was it true? What did being mates even mean? The whole concept was still strange to her.

"What's the matter?" His mood shifted, and his eyes turned dark. "Tell me. Please. You're not regretting this, are you?"

"What?"

"The things I told you last night ... not a lot of people know because they wouldn't understand." His entire body stiffened, and his hold on her loosened. "I've done things ... caused so much pain."

"Damon, no. Oh no." She cupped his face. "Look at me. I may not understand what it's like, but you can't keep blaming yourself for what happened to the men under your command. They knew the risks, and you had bad information."

"But—"

"Damon, you know sometimes guilt can eat you up from the

inside, and the thing about it is, you don't even know it's happening." She laid her head on his shoulder. "You have to learn to forgive yourself, too, before you're consumed by that darkness." Her chest ached for him so bad.

His body relaxed, and his hand soothed her back. "I don't know about that ..." He sighed. "Can we talk about something else? Like what's bothering *you*?"

His questions caught her off guard. "I just ... I ..."

He had told her everything about himself last night, about his past, and yet, he knew nothing about her. About *her* past and what exactly brought her here. That bag of cash still sitting in the trunk of her car was only the tip of the iceberg.

"Anna Victoria?"

"Sorry ... woolgathering." She shifted uncomfortably. "Damon, don't you want to know more about me ... you know, before deciding that I'm your mate?"

"I can't 'decide' you're my mate," he began. "You just are."

"Yes, but there's so much about me you don't know. Like, about my past."

"That doesn't matter to me, none of that does."

Oh Lord, why was he making this harder by being so nice about it? "But you should probably know more about me. Like, about how I got here and my ... my fiancé."

"*Ex*-fiancé," he reminded her not-so-gently.

There was a fierceness in his eyes that made her pull back from him.

He must have realized she was frightened, as his voice turned soft. "Sweetheart, I'm sorry ..." He brushed her cheek. "It's just that ... us shifters, males especially, we get very possessive about our mates. Even thinking of another man with you is driving my bear crazy."

"It does?"

"Yeah. Remember all those times at HQ? When Gabriel or

any other man was around you? I was so jealous I couldn't think straight."

"But Gabriel is your friend," she said. "And those other men are your rangers."

"It doesn't matter. To my animal, they're all rivals." His jaw hardened. "That's why I acted like an ass to you since you came to work for me. And if I haven't yet, I need to apologize for my actions. For chewing you out for no goddamned reason and saying all those mean things to you, all because I was jealous. I didn't mean any of them."

She tried to put herself in his situation, and the truth was, when she thought of him with any other woman, she too felt that hot stab of jealousy. "I think I understand."

"Then you know why I don't wanna hear about this other asshole who loved you enough to ask you to marry him."

Her chest ached at the truth she was hiding from him. "Damon, it's not what you—"

"Don't," his voice was raspy and low. "It doesn't matter. None of it does. Stay here in Blackstone with me. Live your life here, not in the past."

Could she really do that? Leave everything behind her, forget it all, and just start a new life? *People do it every day*, she told herself. She hated that there was this thing between them, not quite a lie, but not quite the truth either. But if he seemed happy not to know ... "All right."

His shoulders relaxed, and he pulled her close, pressing his forehead to hers. "I don't deserve you, but the truth is, I can't let anyone else have you."

A shiver went through her at the possessive, primal words. And darn if it didn't make her *hot*.

"You getting wet, sweetheart?"

She gasped. "How did you—"

"I can smell you," he growled. "And you smell incredible."

ALICIA MONTGOMERY

"No way—oh!" He scooped her up and planted her on his lap. "Damon ..."

Shoving a hand into her hair, he pulled her face down to his so it was centimeters away. "Do you like that? Like it when I get all possessive?"

"N-no," she denied, but the tremble in her voice gave her away. Truth was, his possessiveness was intoxicating and hot.

He chuckled low. "No need to pretend." His teeth nipped at her lips, making her whimper. "You're mine, Anna Victoria. Body and soul." Fingers dug into her scalp, making her body tremble with need.

"Damon, let's go back inside."

His head bent down to her neck, pressing a kiss there before grazing his teeth against her skin. "How about we stay out here instead?"

"Here?"

"Yes. There's no one else around."

A thrill of excitement ran down her spine as he pushed his hips up at her. He was already hard, the head of his cock brushing against her hip. Maneuvering herself so her knees were on either side of him, she reached down to ease his pajamas bottoms off and grasped his length so she could point the tip at her entrance.

"Christ ... sweetheart you're so tight." He let out a strangled sound as she sank down on him.

Lord, she had never felt so full in her life. *Take it slow*, she said to herself, exhaling as she continued to take him in. When she was fully around him, she sighed with relief.

"So good ... mine. My mate."

The blanket fell down to the floor, and though the initial blast of chill made her yelp, his arms winding around her made up for it. Slowly, she began to move, sliding up his length and then sinking back down.

"That's it, sweetheart," he encouraged. "Take it all in. You know you want it."

Her hands braced on his shoulders as she moved her hips, grinding them forward and backward. His breath came in short pants, and the hand in her hair pulled her back to expose her neck. His mouth immediately went to her pulse, his teeth sinking into the skin of her neck. It wasn't enough to break the skin, but it set off something in her she couldn't name.

With a sharp cry, she hauled herself onto her knees and began to bounce on top of him, taking him in long, fast strokes, gripping him as tight as she could. That only seemed to urge him on, and he ripped the front of the shirt she was wearing so he could take a nipple into his mouth.

All the sensations were too much, and her brain was surely going to short circuit. She continued her pace, riding him as hard as she could.

"That's it. Come," he growled against her breast. "You're mine. Say my name when you come."

"I'm ... yours." Closing her eyes, she dug her fingers into his shoulders, but he seemed to enjoy the pain of her nails biting into him as he bit at her nipple and met her hips with upward thrusts. Finally, she felt near the edge as fireworks danced in front of her eyelids. Her body convulsed with her orgasm, clamping tight around him. "Damon!"

He let out a low, primal grunt as his arms hooked under her arms and grasped her shoulders to bring her down hard as he thrust upwards, filling her deep. She felt his cock pulse and flood her inside with his warmth. Another guttural sound escaped his mouth as he nipped her playfully on the ear before settling her again on his lap.

"Ohhh." She couldn't help the long, satisfied sigh that left her lips. The pleased rumble from his chest vibrated against hers deliciously. "Hmmm ... sorry, that was too good."

"Don't be sorry for *that*." He kissed her hair. "I don't think I can get enough of you."

After last night, she wouldn't have believed him except he was still hard inside her right now, like he was still ready for another round. Not that it would be a bad thing.

"Can't get enough of me too, huh?" He teased as a hand moved lower to cup her bottom. "Don't worry, I'll make sure you're satisfied. Everywhere."

His fingers moved close to her center and ...

Her eyes rolled back so far into her head, she was practically blind. "Oh, Damon!"

———

After spending Saturday night at Damon's, she had him drive her back to J.D.'s because she didn't have any more clothes. It simply wouldn't do to show up at the station together, and her wearing wrinkled clothes from Saturday; after all, things had to look professional at work. However, Damon had told her that everybody probably knew that they were mates by now and that it would be no problem, but she insisted, and he didn't argue.

Frankly, she wanted to see if this would last—that feeling that everything was *right*. Though she was afraid she would only feel it when he was around, she wanted to know now, before things got too serious. However, the moment he pulled out of the driveway, she was already missing him and couldn't wait to see him again the next day. Was this what it was like with one's mate? This feeling like she was missing a limb when he wasn't around?

Monday morning came, and excitement thrummed in her veins as she entered the Blackstone Rangers headquarters. She'd already spied his truck in his parking space, so she knew he was in. After planting her things on top of her desk, she grabbed a file folder and knocked on the door.

"Come in," came the curt reply.

Pushing the door open, she padded in quietly.

Damon's head whipped up, and the scowl that usually marred his face dissolved. "You're early," he said, amused. Though his jaw was cleanly shaved this morning, she couldn't forget how his scruff tickled her skin, well, everywhere.

"Am I?" His gaze full-on blazed with desire, and heat pulsed in her. "Damon ... not here," she warned.

A dark brow lifted up. "What did I do?"

"You *know.*" She smirked at him and planted a hand on her hip.

Slowly, calmly, he put the pen in his hand on the desk and then stood up, circling the desk to stalk toward her. With those green eyes, which reminded her of jades, piercing into her, she did, indeed, feel like prey. "I would say you started it."

"How?"

"By being so sexy this morning."

She put her hand on her chest in mock astonishment. "Chief, is that any way to talk to your employees? I should call HR—oh!"

Strong arms encircled her and pulled her to his chest. "I like it when you call me chief."

"You do?"

"Mm-hmm." He flipped her around, pressing her bottom to his groin, where she could feel his semi-hardness against her. "Makes me want to bend you over that table and—"

"Damon!" she admonished, pulling away from him. Still, she couldn't stop the smile turning up the corner of her lips. She liked this playful side of him. "I told you, we need to be professional here. What if someone walked in?"

"I suppose you're right." The heat in his gaze could have

scorched her panties right off. "Being my assistant, I think we should work late tonight. I'll need your ... assistance on a few things."

"Ha." She pushed the folder in her hand at him. "Sign these please, so I can send them over to requisitions."

"Yes, ma'am. But first," he snaked a hand around her waist. "One kiss."

"Oh, all right." The folder dropped to the floor as soon as his mouth descended on hers. Her body sang as their lips touched, as it had been years—and not hours—since they last kissed. He ravished her mouth thoroughly, and when he was done, she had to brace herself against his chest to keep her balance. "Oh my."

He grinned at her boyishly, then picked up the folder. "See you at lunch?"

Straightening her blouse and her hair, she gave him a nod. "See you then." She turned on her heel and walked out of the office.

As she sat back at her desk, she couldn't help but glance at the clock. Though she managed to do most of her work, it felt like the time crawled by. Finally, five minutes before twelve, the door to Damon's office flew open.

"Ready?" he asked.

Her hands gripped the side of her desk to keep her from flying out of her seat. "I am," she said, grabbing her brown paper bag. As she walked around her desk, to her surprise, he took her hand in his.

"Let's go to the cafeteria."

Despite knowing she should take her hand from his, she couldn't do it. So, instead, she braced herself as they walked through the building on their way to the cafeteria. However, she should have trusted Damon more. No one seemed to bat an eye that the chief and his assistant were walking together hand in hand. Maybe there were one or two double takes, as if they couldn't believe what they were seeing, but no one sent them nasty looks or made any mean comments.

When they reached the cafeteria, they sat down at an empty table, and moments later, Gabriel, Daniel, and even Anders joined them. None of the guys said anything, though Gabriel did wink at her, and Anders didn't say anything flirtatious or inappropriate throughout the whole hour.

The week went by much quicker than she anticipated. She slept over at his cabin almost every night, except for one disastrous time when they tried to stay over in her room at J.D.'s place. After they had dinner at an Italian place he suggested, she insisted on going back to her room. Unfortunately, the tiny single bed barely fit them both, plus J.D. had rapped on the wall in the middle of the night, yelling, "I'm trying to sleep here, you horny *ef-fers!*" They'd stayed at his place since then.

It would have been nice to sleep in on Saturday morning, especially after Friday night, when Damon cooked dinner for her and they made love for hours after. However, she'd already promised the girls she would do her first yoga class that weekend, and aside from the initial six women, another three planned to join them.

The prospect that she might actually be able to turn this into a business made her giddy with excitement. So, though she was loath to leave Damon's warm bed—not to mention the man himself—she drove to Blackstone Castle early that morning. They made plans to meet up later that day, as she wanted to do some shopping on Main Street without having to worry about his anxiety over crowds. They settled on an early dinner at Rosie's as the weather predicted heavy snowfall later that night, and she didn't want to be out driving when that happened.

"Wow." It was difficult not to gasp as she pulled up the driveway toward Blackstone Castle. Catherine hadn't been kidding. It really was a real-life fairy-tale castle in the mountains, complete with turrets. Turning her engine off, she got out of the car and headed to the front entrance. Before she could even knock, the door opened.

"Hello, you made it," Catherine greeted. "Thanks for coming early. Only Amelia and Georgina are here, so we can help if you need to make any changes to the layout I did."

"Hey, Catherine. Yeah, the directions were easy and you're actually closer to Damon's than J.D's place." A blush crept into her cheeks when the other woman gave her a knowing look. "So … nice castle."

Catherine stepped aside to let her in. "Yeah, we do what we can. Come on," she cocked her head. "I'll tell you what I know about the history."

They chatted as they made their way through the elegantly-designed halls of Blackstone Castle. Everything about it screamed old money, from the plush Persian carpets to the art hanging on the wall. It was like stepping back in time and visiting with the Rockefellers or Vanderbilts.

"… so, Lucas Lennox promised the countess he'd build her a castle if she would marry him," Catherine finished and then gestured for her to go through to the next room first.

"And so he did." This place was mind-boggling, and she had grown up in a six-bedroom mansion in Albuquerque's most exclusive neighborhood. "This is perfect," she said when they entered the large, well-lit room and walked toward where a small table was set up and Georgina and Amelia were chatting. Like the rest of the castle, the ballroom was richly-decorated with hardwood floors, large windows, intricate woodwork molding, and several crystal chandeliers. She could imagine it filled with people in tuxedos and ballgowns, maybe an orchestra on the side. Today, however, it was completely empty save for the yoga mats arranged on the floor, and two rambunctious children—a boy and a girl—running around the expansive space.

"... can't catch me!" The boy shouted at the girl. He looked to be about six or seven while the girl was probably younger.

"Yes, I can!" she shouted back as she chased after him.

"Grayson! Cassie!" Georgina Lennox called. "Stop running around please!"

The two children stopped in their tracks. "Aww, Mom!" the boy—Grayson—complained. "We were having fun."

"No fair!" Cassie added, crossing her arms over her chest. "I was about to catch him."

"Our yoga class is about to start, Grayson," Georgina warned. "I told you, you could come and play with Cassie, but you have to stay out of the way when we begin, okay? Now come here." The two kids trudged over to them. "Anna Victoria," she began. "This is my son, Grayson."

"And this," Amelia ruffled the little girl's head, "is my daughter, Cassie. Say hello, kids."

"Hello, Miss Anna Victoria," they said in unison.

Anna Victoria bent down to their eye level. "Nice to meet you."

"Grayson," Georgina began. "Why don't you and Cassie go up to the nursery? Uncle Matthew and Devon should be there. He said he'd look after you guys while we're at class."

"Okay!" Grayson said with a nod, then took Cassie's hand. "C'mon, Cass, maybe Uncle Matthew'll fly us today." With that the two children dashed out of the ballroom.

"They're adorable," she said to the two women.

"But they sure are a handful," Georgina said.

"Do you like children?" Amelia asked Anna Victoria.

"I guess?" She hadn't been around many kids, having been an only child. But she supposed they were asking about her and

Damon, and that made her stomach flutter. Was it too early to think about that?

"Ahem." Georgina cleared her throat as she and Amelia smiled at each other knowingly. "Looks like we should get started," she nodded behind them, where J.D., Kate, and a couple of other women were filing in.

"Ah, right." With a deep breath, she turned around. "Hello, ladies! Good morning." *I can do this*, she told herself. This was something she wanted to go right. "My name is Anna Victoria, thanks for coming."

Kate began to introduce the other three women. "This is Nepheli," she nodded at the tall brunette. "She works with my husband and Christina at the Marketing Department at Lennox."

"How do you do?" she asked, her voice heavily accented.

"And this," she gestured to the petite redhead, "is Penny Walker, Amelia's sister-in-law."

"Hi." Penny waved at her shyly. "I've never done yoga, but I'm excited to try it."

"Finally," she gestured to the other redhead in the trio, "this is Dutchy Forrester, Blackstone's premiere fashion designer."

Dutchy smiled and rolled her eyes. "Kate tends to exaggerate things, but you probably already know that."

"I'm glad I finally got you out of the house, Dutch," Kate said. "Even if I did have to drag you out."

"It's lovely to meet you ladies," Anna Victoria said. "Why don't we begin?"

They all headed toward the mats in the middle of the ballroom, with Anna Victoria taking the one at the front, and the others assembled behind her.

She led them through an easy flow, not really knowing what everyone's levels were, but made sure to give tips and modifications for both beginners and advanced students.

"That's it," she encouraged as she showed Penny how to get into the downward dog position properly. "I know it's not easy, but don't worry about getting it perfect. Everyone has to start somewhere. Honor where you are in your process."

Continuing through the series of movements, she shifted between showing them what to do and walking around to help them. "That's it, ladies. Don't be discouraged if you can't do everything today. You might not be able to do it now, but a week or a few weeks from now, who knows what you'll be able to do if you put your mind to it?"

Finally, they neared the end, and she had everyone lie down on their mats. "Relax your body. One part at a time. Focus on your breathing. Release the tension in your muscles." After a few more minutes of silence, she took a deep breath, then sat up. "All right, ladies, and we are done. Thank you so much." She put her hands together and nodded at them.

"I feel awesome," Christina said. "God, I needed that so bad."

"I thought I was going to fall over," Georgina laughed. "But you were such a good teacher."

Everyone came up to her to praise and thank her. The fact that she was able to finish the class and help people made her feel euphoric. It was an incredible feeling, and deep inside, she realized that this was what she was meant to do.

"Now, how about brunch?" Catherine offered. "I have food set up in the dining room." All the women agreed heartily and followed her out of the ballroom.

As they sat and ate, Anna Victoria used the time to get to know them, as well as ask the women what she could do to improve the classes. They were all helpful, and all wanted to come back next week, plus suggested she offer more types of classes or later schedules, since they had friends who had wanted to come but simply couldn't make it on a Saturday morning. She told them she would take that into consideration, if Catherine was amenable to hosting them at another time, which of course she said was definitely possible.

"So, it's nice to see you again," J.D. said as they all began to file out of the castle.

"Oh. Sorry," she said, embarrassed. They hadn't seen each other or even talked since Monday. "I've been, uh, busy."

"Or getting busy?" she teased. "Hey, don't worry about it, I'm kidding. I'm so happy for you, Anna Victoria. I really am. And I'm so glad Damon's found you."

"You are?"

"Yeah, he's been ... well you know the last couple of years haven't been great, but I know things are already improving with him, and I know it's all because of you."

"I wouldn't say it's all me," she replied. "But you're right. There is something different about him." Gone was the sullen, cold man she'd first met. Sure, he was still the same disciplined, responsible, and organized boss at work, but he seemed more approachable now.

"But I am mad at him for hogging you. I miss you so much," J.D. said. "What're you planning to do now?"

"Maybe head to Main Street for some shopping?" The envelope that Catherine handed her after the class was another reason to celebrate—finally some extra cash so she could purchase some luxury items. "And then meet up with Damon at Rosie's."

"Why don't we head to South Blackstone instead?" J.D. suggested. "They have more shops nowadays, and we can look at some space for you."

"Space?" she asked, puzzled.

"Duh, for your fitness studio."

She laughed. "Oh goodness, I've only taught one class."

"It's not a bad idea, though, right?" J.D. elbowed her.

"You're not going to sign up for a lease right this moment, but we can at least imagine it, right?"

Did she dare think about it? This morning's class had her fired up. It was like she hadn't known she'd wanted to do this, but now, she was excited, and it would be nice to have something of her own—kinda like J.D. had with her garage. "All right, let's go."

# Chapter 11

Anna Victoria followed J.D. in her car all the way to South Blackstone, a new high-end development just on the outskirts of the main town center. It was obvious that Blackstone was growing and prospering, and she was glad they decided to expand instead of replacing the older parts of town. She rather liked the quaint area around Main Street, but South Blackstone did have more shops, cafes, and restaurants that were hipper and more international.

They browsed through the different shops, and J.D. convinced her to stop and look at spaces that had a For Rent sign outside, and imagined which place would be most suitable, and how a studio could be set up. Starting her own business wasn't something she was planning on doing right this moment, but it was nice to dream.

She was exhausted by the time they finished and drove to Rosie's. The temperature had dropped considerably by then and so she was eager to get some dinner and go back to Damon's place before it got too bad. However, J.D. had invited herself, and since she hadn't seen Gabriel in a while, asked him to come, too. He was already there by the time they entered.

"Hello, ladies," Rosie greeted from where she stood at the hostess station. "And, Gabriel," she added with a nod. "Back again?"

"You know I love it here," he said.

"This is the fourth time this week," she noted, then looked at Anna Victoria. "Damon joining you?"

*I guess everyone knows about us*, she mused. "Yes, he should be here any—oh."

On cue, Damon appeared at the entrance, his face drawn into a frown. Anna Victoria tensed, sensing his apprehension at being inside the restaurant, even if it was early and only half occupied.

"You made it," she said as she walked to him and took his hand, giving it a squeeze.

His face immediately changed, and those mesmerizing jade eyes fixed on her. "Of course I did. How was class?"

"It was great!" She proceeded to tell him the short version about her successful first ever real stint as a yoga teacher. "But, I can tell you more later. C'mon, let's sit down. I'm starving." She cocked her head at her two companions. "J.D. kinda invited herself and Gabriel. I hope you don't mind."

"Not at all, I haven't seen J.D. in a while." He greeted his two friends, and Rosie led them to a booth.

"Okay, kids," Rosie began. "You know the drill. However, our new flavors for today are truffle cheese, spicy samosa, and Earl Grey cream." She turned to Gabriel. "You'll want one each of those, I suppose?"

He nodded. "Yes, please."

Damon raised a brow, but didn't comment on Gabriel's order. "I'll have the dinner special, Rosie."

"Me too," Anna Victoria said. "I'll let you know what dessert I want later, if that's okay?"

"Me three," J.D. added. "Though I want to try that Earl Grey one, and I know Gabriel won't give me even one bite."

"You bet," Gabriel said smugly. "Keep your hands off my dessert, McNamara."

Rosie chuckled. "All right, kids, sit tight. I'll have those to ya soon."

"Can't wait," Gabriel called out. "Truffle cheese ... samosa ... Earl Grey," he said, with a dreamy look on his face. "I already know it's going to be good."

"Do you even know what a samosa is?" J.D. asked.

"Of course I do," Gabriel said, miffed. "I'm not an uncultured swine, you know."

Anna Victoria laughed. "Maybe I should have tried it too. I haven't had Indian food in a long time."

"I know a place in Verona Mills," Damon suggested as he linked his fingers through hers under the table. "We can go there for dinner tomorrow if you'd like."

"That would be nice," she said. One of the things she'd bought was a nice dress—on sale, of course—and it would be perfect for a date night.

Anna Victoria enjoyed herself immensely during the rest of dinner. Obviously, the three had a dynamic that was built on years of friendship, but they never made her feel like an outsider or excluded. They explained all their private jokes, and told embarrassing stories about Damon, much to his chagrin. Truly, it was the perfect day. Blackstone was not just growing on her, but she was starting to really feel at home here. Great friends, great job, great guy—what more could she want?

"Everything good?" Rosie asked as she stopped by to check on them.

"God, Rosie," Gabriel said as he licked his spoon clean. "What do you put in this? I can't get enough."

"Jeez, Russel, do you need to be alone with that thing?" J.D.

asked. "Although I have to agree, this new stuff is amazing, Rosie."

"It's all thanks to my new employee." Rosie jerked her thumb toward the kitchen. "Talented one when it comes to pastries."

Gabriel's head swung toward where she was pointing. "New employee, huh?"

"Yeah. Hardworking too. Comes in early, gets stuff done lickety-split. Anyway, anything else I can get ya?"

"Just the bill, Rosie, thank you," Damon said.

"You got it."

He turned to Anna Victoria. "How about we—" A ringing sound interrupted him. With a frown, he fished his phone from his pocket. "Cooper," he said in that authoritative voice he used when he was at work. "Yeah?" As he listened to the other caller, his brows drew closer together. "All right. I'll be there as soon as I can." Putting the phone away, he massaged his temples. "Sorry about that. I'm needed back at HQ."

"Oh no," Anna Victoria said. "Is it serious?"

"Not sure yet. Moose shifter got himself injured badly. Fell down the side of a cliff. I have to coordinate getting him to the hospital. I'm sorry, sweetheart, looks like we'll have to take a rain check for tonight."

"Damon, that's standard stuff, something you can have Rogers do, since he's on duty tonight," Gabriel pointed out. "You need to learn to delegate, man. And you know Rogers likes the responsibility. He's been dying to prove himself so he can get that promotion."

Damon seemed conflicted, so he turned to Anna Victoria. "I'm sorry, sweetheart. It might take all night. But if you'd rather have me stay home—"

"It's all right." She squeezed his hand. It was disappointing that she was going to spend the night alone, but she knew how much the job meant to him. "Do what you need to do."

He leaned down and brushed his lips to hers. "I'll make it up to you, I swear."

"Since you won't be back until morning, why don't you crash back at my place?" J.D. offered. "We can have a girl's night. Besides, you don't want her driving by herself in the dark up those roads in her car in this weather." She nodded out the window. The snowfall was already starting.

"Are you all right with that, Anna Victoria?" he asked.

"Of course," she said, with a smile at J.D. It wasn't how she imagined the evening to go, but spending more time with J.D. wasn't so bad. In truth, being around her and the girls today had been nice; she felt like she truly was putting down roots in Blackstone. She could survive one night without Damon. Heck, she might not even miss him.

"I gotta run." Damon got up and put some bills on the table. "Dinner's on me," he said before leaning down to kiss her.

A thrill ran up her spine as his lips touched hers. Okay, so maybe she would miss this. And his body that was hot as H-E-double sippy straws. *Oh God, I've turned into a sex addict.*

"*Ahem*, guys," J.D. said wryly. "There are kids here."

"And people trying to eat," Gabriel added.

Damon cleared his throat. "I'll swing by tomorrow as soon as I can."

"Stay safe," she called after him. He gave her a wave as he headed for the exit.

"Ooh, you got it bad," J.D. said with a laugh.

She couldn't help the smile tugging up her lips even if she tried. "Is it that obvious?" Was it possible that in such a short time, she had fallen in love with Damon? "Oh God."

*I love him.*

*I love him!*

"You don't have to say it twice," J.D. laughed.

"Oh Lord, I said that part out loud?" She buried her face in her hands. "Is it too soon? Should I tell him? Or will that scare him away?"

Gabriel chuckled. "Soon? Are you kidding me? He was halfway in love with you when you walked in the door at The Den."

"Are you ... sure? I mean, it's not just because of the mate thing? I mean, what does it even mean, mates?"

"Don't look at us," Gabriel said, raising his palms. "I mean, I know we're shifters, but neither of us are mated."

"It's supposed to be a special bond," J.D. said. "I don't know much either, since we shifters are private about that kind of thing. And I heard it's different for each one. Anyway, I'm so happy for you. And maybe just a tiny part of me is being selfish here, because that means you really aren't going away now," she said smugly. "Now come on, this might be the last night I get to hang out with you. Let's get outta here."

All three of them got up and headed out to the parking lot. Gabriel walked over to his Jeep, a few cars down from J.D.'s truck. "I'll see you girls—sonofabitch!" he exclaimed.

"What's wrong?" J.D. asked.

He bent down to inspect the front driver's side tire. Its bottom half looked flatter than a pancake.

"Hmm ... that's not the only one." J.D. cocked her head at the rear one, which was also deflated. When Gabriel saw it, he rounded the car.

"They've all been slashed," he groaned as he came around from the other side of the Jeep. "Who the fuck would do this?"

"Probably some punk kids," J.D. said. "You got a spare?"

"Of course I do, but just one. Goddammit." He raked his fingers through his hair. "What the fuck am I supposed to do?"

J.D. rolled her eyes. "All right, calm your tits, drama king."

She turned to Anna Victoria. "Why don't you run on home? I got some donuts back at the shop. We can get this done quick, but you shouldn't have to wait around for us."

"Are you sure?" she asked.

"Yeah. You had a long day. Get showered and into your pajamas. Pick a couple of movies on Netflix and find some cheesy ones we can make fun of."

"Ha! Will do!" She gave J.D. the thumbs-up. "Sorry about your tires, Gabriel."

"Yeah, yeah," Gabriel groaned. "Drive safe, Anna Victoria."

Getting into her Mercedes, she turned the engine on and drove out to Main Street. Soon, she was pulling into the familiar driveway of J.D.'s house, parked in the empty spot next to the garage, then got out of her car.

A chill passed through her. "Brrr ..." Tightening her coat around herself, she hopped up the porch steps. However, when she reached for the knob, the door was already ajar. *Strange.* J.D. would never leave the door unlocked. Or open.

"Hello, Anna Victoria."

Ice froze in her veins. *No. Oh God, no. But how—*

"What? Did you think you could hide from me forever?" The voice made her skin crawl, as it always did. "You know I'd find you anywhere."

Her gut tightened in knots as she slowly turned around. "Mr. Jameson."

"Tsk, tsk? So formal with your fiancé?"

Edward Jameson stepped forward, a cool smile on his face. He wasn't an overly tall man, maybe an inch shy of six feet, with patrician features and a full head of hair that was silvering at the temples. Most people would call him handsome or distinguished, but there was always an edge to him—a cruel smirk to his mouth or sharpness in his eyes that no one else seemed to notice except her. As usual, he was accompanied by two menacing-looking men in dark suits. They stood like silent sentinels beside him, neither one speaking or reacting as they remained alert, ready to pounce at any sign of danger.

"W-what are you doing here?"

"What am I doing here?" he sneered. "You didn't think you could get away from me that easily, did you?"

"I left a note." Okay that sounded pathetic, but it's not like they were in love or even in a relationship. "I told my father I couldn't go through with the wedding."

"Couldn't go through with it?" he mocked.

"If you want your—your bag, you can have it." she said. "It's in the trunk of my car." She couldn't bear to touch it, even to take it out, knowing where that money came from.

"So that's where it was," he said. "We searched everywhere in the house."

"Let me get it for you, and then you can leave."

"Leave?" he scoffed. "Have you forgotten that we had an agreement? Marry me and your father's debts would be forgiven."

Her stomach roiled. How could she have agreed to such a thing? Well, she had no choice, after all. Her father had made that very clear, that night when she walked into his study.

She had been shocked when he told her she had to marry Jameson. "You're ... you're just trading me? Like I'm some sort of object? You're joking right? Are we in the Dark Ages? You can't—" The slap had come so fast; the shock had silenced her. The sting came right after, but it couldn't have hurt her more than his words.

"Listen, you spoiled little bitch," he snarled. "I've clothed you, fed you, paid for everything for twenty-five years so you could run around with your friends and party your life away. The way I see it, I *own* you, and if I want to trade you away, I can do it. Besides, if you say no, then you can say goodbye to everything—this house, your car, your credit cards, because my creditors will come in here and start hauling it all away. You will marry him, Anna Victoria," he said. "You owe me."

What could she have said at that moment? Her whole world was collapsing. She had no job, no prospects, what could she do?

The very next day, she met her "groom" at his house for dinner with him and her father. *At least he wasn't old and decrepit,* she had thought, though Edward Jameson was probably twenty years older than her. However, the moment he laid eyes on her, she already felt *dirty.* He launched right into wedding preparations, and it seemed everything had already been planned, from the ceremony to the reception venue, even her gown. All she had to do was show up.

But as the wedding drew closer, she knew deep in her heart something was wrong. Plus, there were whispers here and there, about Jameson's connections to the cartels down south. A few days before the wedding, she scrounged up all her courage to go to his penthouse on Central Avenue to tell him she wasn't going to marry him.

However, he probably wasn't expecting her show up one late one evening. From where she stood in the entryway, she could hear the shouts and harsh words, but she walked right in anyway. Jameson was there, but he wasn't alone. Aside from his two bodyguards, there was a fourth person—a short and balding man she had recognized as the local police chief. She quickly apologized and excused herself, and dashed out.

The next day, Jameson acted like nothing had happened, but he did have one of his bodyguards put a large duffel bag in the trunk of his car. *The* duffel bag.

Then the morning of the wedding came and she saw the headline on her phone's news alert notification: Police Chief Suspected of Bribery Found Dead in the Desert. Her instincts screamed at her, and she immediately went to retrieve the bag in the trunk of her car. She could barely open it because her hands shook so bad, but when she did and saw the cash, it all connected and clicked in her brain; there was no way she could marry Jameson.

His scornful voice knocked her out of her reverie. "I don't have time for this. You're mine, bought and paid for, and you're coming back with me. Tonight."

"Coming with you? Are you going to tie me up and take me forcibly?"

"If I have to." His tone was serious. "But I know you'll come with me. Unless you want something to happen to your dear old daddy."

She flinched visibly. While it was David's fault she was in this mess, she didn't hate him enough to want him dead. And she already knew what Jameson was capable of. Her throat burned with unshed tears, but she wasn't going to give him the satisfaction.

The sound of an approaching vehicle made her start. She thought it was J.D., but no, it was a different truck, a familiar dark blue one.

*Damon.*

But it couldn't be! He was going to be gone until tomorrow, he said.

"Oh look, it's your boyfriend." His dark brows snapped together. "Now what is he doing here? I thought I saw him leave the restaurant."

Her jaw dropped. "You saw—"

"Don't look surprised, darling." The way he said that term of endearment made her skin crawl. "I tracked you down a week ago, and I've had eyes on you since then. Why do you think I had your other friend's tires slashed? I couldn't risk him coming back here with you. We could have taken on your little mechanic friend, but he would have made things messy. Wouldn't want to hurt the precious heir to the Russel fortune." His eyes turned sharp as flint. "Are you screwing him, too? Maybe I should have had you when I had the chance. Here I was, being a gentleman, giving you space and letting you decide when to come to my bed. And then you go and fuck the first cock that comes your way."

She drew in a sharp breath as the truck's engine quieted and the headlights turned off. *Do something*, her brain screamed.

"I should kill him for touching you, but I don't have time. Just get rid of him," Jameson ordered. "You know what I'm capable of." He nodded at his two bodyguards, who discreetly patted the guns she knew were holstered under those suits. "Tell him we're going for a drive to talk things through."

Terror gripped her chest, rendering her unable to make a sound. So, she just nodded.

The truck door opened, and Damon stepped out. As he walked up the driveway, her heart leapt at the sight of his familiar, strong frame. She allowed herself to drink it all in—his handsome face, that tiny dent in the middle of his chin. Those strong arms that held her and kept her safe. No, she couldn't let him die. She loved him too much.

"Anna Victoria, I—" He stopped as he was halfway up the porch steps. That unnerving green gaze of his zeroed in on Jameson. "What's going on here?"

## Chapter 12

Damon had been halfway to HQ when he realized he was making a mistake. Each minute that passed that he wasn't with Anna Victoria was one he regretted. Gabriel had been right—there was nothing extraordinary about the situation with the moose shifter. So, he called Daniel and told him to handle it, then turned his truck around to go back to Anna Victoria.

The snowfall had picked up considerably, so he had to be careful as he drove back to town. He was thinking of what to say to her, how to express what was happening inside of him. As he neared J.D.'s place, he felt more alive. And at the same time, more at peace.

Anna Victoria quieted that part of his soul that was restless, calmed The Demon, and made his life more vibrant. Though he'd never felt it before, he was pretty sure he was head over heels for her.

Which was why the moment he saw that other man with her on J.D.'s porch, his stomach sank, and his chest filled with hot, searing jealousy. The Demon rose again, its claw ready for action.

"What's going on here?"

"Damon," she began. "This is Edward Jameson."

Two large men in expensive suits flanked another older, smaller man in an even more expensive suit. From the tips of his well-polished leather shoes to the top of his slicked-back hair, he oozed that rich, *I-can-buy-you-ten-times-over* presence. Hell, he even *smelled* expensive. "Who the hell are you?"

"I'm her fiancé," the prick said smugly.

Blood roared in his ears as a growl rattled from deep within. The Demon was raking its mighty claws against its human prison, eager to get at this rival male. Damon, too, wanted to rip this fucking guy's head off. He turned to Anna Victoria. "Is this true?"

Jameson cleared his throat. "I said—"

"I wasn't talking to you, asshole." His voice had turned inhuman, and he couldn't help feeling satisfied to see the other man's face flash briefly with fear and surprise before that smarmy mask slipped back on. "Anna Victoria? What is he doing here?"

"He came to see me," she said. "He wants to talk."

"About *what*?"

"I came to take her home," Jameson said.

"*Over my dead body!*" Rage filled every corner of his body. He was sorely tempted to let The Demon out, but murder was still illegal, after all. Still, it took every ounce of control to leash back the creature that wanted to shred this man to pieces.

"Why don't you ask her, then?" Jameson's beady eyes zeroed in on Anna Victoria. "Darling?"

"I made a mistake leaving him at the altar." Her eyes darted around. "Mr.—Edward and I are going to go for a drive to work things out. You should go."

He couldn't believe his ears. "Anna Victoria—"

"I said, *go*. Please." Her face turned away from him, focusing on Jameson. "Just ... leave, Damon."

A knife-like pain sliced deep into his gut. "You can't mean that."

"I-I do." She still wouldn't look at him. "Leave, Damon. We can talk about this in the morning."

"You leave with him now, and you won't hear from me again."

Her eyes closed. "Fine."

A crushing sensation wrapped around his rib cage, making it difficult to breathe. He couldn't move a muscle. Couldn't make a sound. Couldn't do anything, as if any attempt to stray from his current position would shatter him into a million pieces. It was unbelievable that he would know the feeling of both love and heartbreak in the span of five minutes.

"Perhaps we should just leave," Edward said. "Darling?"

She nodded, and he draped an arm around her, leading her away from him. It was like a movie playing in his mind, as if he was detached from the whole thing, watching her—his mate—walk away from him and choose another man.

He didn't even realize the three black SUVs had peeled away, the screeches of their tires a shrill disturbance in the silence of the evening. No, he simply stood there for what seemed like eternity, letting thick white flakes of snow blanket around him and melt on his face.

The light of an oncoming vehicle jolted him out of his trance. The truck stopped in the empty spot next to the Mercedes, and J.D. hopped out, Gabriel following her from the passenger's side.

"Hey, Damon," she greeted cheerfully. "I'm glad you changed your mind! Guess who got his tires slashed? Didn't have enough spares, so I told him, why not bunker down and join us for girls' night? We can braid his—Damon?" A frown marred her face. "What's wrong?"

"Damon." Gabriel dashed to his side. "Damon, what's the matter?"

How could he explain? He couldn't even form the words in his mouth. "She left."

"She left?" J.D. asked incredulously. "Who? Anna Victoria?"

He managed a nod.

"Where did she go?" Gabriel asked.

"Home."

"Home?" he echoed. "What do you mean, home?"

"To Albuquerque," he said. "Or she will. Anyway, she'll explain everything to you when she comes back with her fiancé." The word coming from his own mouth made him want to retch. "They went for a drive. To talk in private."

"Fiancé?" J.D. exclaimed.

"Yeah. Showed up here. Said they were going to work things out."

"And how the hell did he even know she was here in Blackstone?" J.D. asked.

"She must have told him where she was." Had they been talking all this time? Was it all a lie then? Being with him? Why the hell would she sleep with him if she was still talking to that bastard?

"Damon, man, I'm sorry," Gabriel began, placing a hand on his shoulder. "I can't even—"

"No!" J.D. stamped her foot down for emphasis.

"No?" Gabriel frowned. "What do you mean, no?"

"No, as in, I don't believe it! She wouldn't leave you to go to another man. She's your mate."

No one would ever call J.D. sweet or naive, but in this instance, Damon was beginning to think those were suitable descriptions for his friend. "It's okay, J.D.," he began. "She fooled us all." *Me, most of all,* he added bitterly.

"There's something wrong here," J.D. insisted. "Damon, you're her mate! What does your bear say?"

A growl vibrated from his chest. The Demon roared, as if telling him that something wasn't right here. *Shut up!* His damned bear was confused. Was this what happened when mates broke up? Would his bear continue on an even deeper spiral?

"Goddammit!" J.D. grabbed his arm. "Damon, Anna Victoria is in love with you. She said so herself after you left Rosie's. Tell her, Gabe."

"She said the words," Gabriel said with a shrug. "But if she left ..."

"No, no, this is wrong." J.D. paced. "I need to think." Pivoting on her heel, she marched up to the front door. "Guys!"

The alarm in J.D.'s voice made his spine straighten. "What's wrong?" he asked.

"The lock ... it's been broken. My house ... holy fuck!"

"What?" Gabriel sprinted up the steps. "Motherfucker, what happened in here?"

Something in his gut flared, and he bounded toward the entrance. "What the—" Disbelief scrambled his brain as he took in the sight before him. The living room had been ransacked—furniture flipped over, couch cushions slashed, keepsakes and books tossed to the ground.

J.D. rushed out of the spare bedroom. "They went through the entire house." Her teeth gritted together and her hands curled into claws. "Motherfuckers."

"What happened, Damon?" Gabriel said. "Tell us."

Did Jameson do this? He hadn't seen it himself, but that bastard did have those two suited bodyguards with him, so they could have done this in no time. He took a cushion off the floor and sniffed it. *Same cologne as Jameson.* He could picture it in his mind—that bastard sitting on the sofa as his henchmen ransacked the place. But why? "Fuck," he cursed.

"Damon," J.D. said. "Tell us what you know. *Now.*"

He went through the story as quickly and succinctly as he could. Really, there wasn't much to tell. He arrived, and Jameson and Anna Victoria were on the porch, and then they left. But as he replayed the events in his mind, he tried to recall more details. How Anna Victoria's voice shook as she spoke. The way she flinched when Jameson put his arm around her. And how she refused to look him in the eye when she told him to go.

"No way she wanted to go with him," Gabriel concluded. "But—" His head turned toward the door, body going stiff as a board. "There's someone out there." Without another word, the lion shifter sprinted out the door.

"What the heck—Gabriel!" J.D. called as she went after him, Damon hot on her heels.

A sharp cry caught their attention, and they ran toward Anna Victoria's car. Gabriel was on the ground, wrestling with a man in a suit. It was no contest, though, as Gabriel quickly put his opponent in a chokehold. "Where is she?" he growled, loosening his grip. "Where did that bastard take her?"

The man said nothing, so Gabriel squeezed his arm around the man's neck again. "Where is she?"

The Demon roared inside Damon, wanting to join in and rip the man's face off.

"Guys!" J.D. exclaimed, pointing to something in the back of Anna Victoria's car. "Look."

Damon turned to the trunk, which had been popped open. A black duffel bag sat inside and bundles of cash peeked out from the open zipper.

"Holy fucking moly," J.D. gasped. "What the hell is that doing in there?"

Damon walked over to Gabriel and his prisoner. "Are you going to talk, motherfucker?" he asked.

"Fuck you," the man said, spittle flying out of his mouth.

It was obvious the man was loyal to Jameson. "Take care of him," he ordered Gabriel.

The lion shifter nodded and tightened his grip until the man passed out. With a disgusted sound, he got up and brushed himself off. "Bastard."

"What are we going to do?" J.D. asked, a worried look on her face. "That asshole fiancé of hers probably kidnapped her."

"And then sent his bodyguard back to get the money," Gabriel added. "What was Anna Victoria doing with this much cash in the trunk of her car? Did she have it all this time?"

"Doesn't matter." A fire blazed in Damon's chest. Anna Victoria was his mate, and anyone who dared take her away would regret it. "The only thing that does matter is getting her back." And for once, he and The Demon were in agreement. "Call P.D.," he said to Gabriel. "Ask their patrols to keep a lookout for three black SUVs heading out of town."

"Will do, Chief." He fished out his phone. "I'll have them pull all security footage around the area too. If they give me grief about it, I'll remind Police Chief Meacham about that large check I wrote for the policeman's fund."

"Damon?" J.D. put a hand on his arm. "Are you okay?"

His brain was focused on a task. And when he was determined to accomplish something, he never gave up. Anna Victoria was *his*. He would get her back, even if he had tear down every town and rip up every road from here to Albuquerque. Turning to J.D., he said, "I've never been better."

# Chapter 13

Hope drained out of Anna Victoria as the minutes ticked by and they drove farther and farther away from J.D.'s house. The look on Damon's face when she told him to leave shattered her heart into pieces, but what could she do? She had to save him. Edward Jameson's ruthlessness knew no bounds. He had a police chief killed, what would he do to Damon?

Marrying Jameson would be a small sacrifice to keep Damon safe.

Still, the idea that Damon hated her made her chest contract with pain. *I love you so much, Damon.*

But he would never hear those words from her. Maybe it would have been better if she never came here in the first place. If she'd never met him and just drove on. Or stayed at home and gone through with the wedding. And by the looks of it, she would have ended up in the same place anyway. Married to a vile man she didn't love.

Not wanting to further wallow in her grief, she instead focused outside. The snow was falling fast. Oh, she would miss the loveliness of the snow in the mountains. Miss the view from Damon's porch. Miss the—

Her thoughts made a complete one-eighty as they passed a familiar road sign. *Welcome to the Blackstone Mountains.*

Her head snapped toward Jameson, who sat beside her in the back seat of the second SUV. "Where are we going?" When he didn't answer, she called the driver's attention. "Are you lost? You're going the wrong way. This isn't the way back to New Mexico."

"No, it's not," Jameson said, his voice completely emotionless.

Dread sank in her stomach, and her limbs felt paralyzed. Despite her chest squeezing the air from her lungs, she managed to say, "You were never planning to take me back to Albuquerque, were you?"

Slowly, Jameson turned to her. "No, darling." The dark, emptiness in his eyes made her skin crawl. "I can't risk it. You're a loose end."

*Oh God.* Fear sank into her chest. "But you can have the money back," she said, panicked. "I didn't spend it. Never even took it out of my car. It's all there."

"But you were there that night," he began. "You saw us, didn't you? Police Chief Ryan and me at the penthouse. You're the only one who can link us before he died."

*You mean, before you killed him,* she wanted to scream, but bit her lip. "I won't say anything. Please. You can have it in writing. If ... if we get married, they can't make me testify against you."

He scoffed. "Too late, Anna Victoria. You shouldn't have left me at the altar and jilted me."

"My father will—"

"No one knows I've tracked you here or that I'm even here now," he interrupted. "According to my private plane's manifest, I'm currently up in Vermont. Your friends back home will simply think you ran away to start a new life, while everyone here will assume you've gone home and reconciled with me. As for your father ... well, he'll be distraught, but it won't matter, because he will never find you." He glanced out the window. "I have to admit, you couldn't have picked a better place to hide from me. A town full of shifters who don't care for anyone but their own," he sneered. "It's the perfect place to get rid of you. Maybe I won't even have to hide your body, and one of these animals will devour what's left of you."

It seemed Jameson had already planned her gruesome fate from the beginning. *God, this was all so hopeless.* Her entire body went numb, her brain still attempting to process the thought that she would die tonight.

They kept on going, driving up unfamiliar roads that took them higher up the mountains. The vehicle had passed the turnoff that led to the station and Damon's house miles ago, which meant they were going farther than she'd ever been before.

"We've driven long enough," Edward told the driver. "I don't see anything but trees and snow up here. You can stop now."

"Yes, sir," the driver replied as the vehicle slowed down. While the SUV behind them halted, the one in the lead continued.

"Call them to come back," Jameson snapped. "Then we can proceed."

Anna Victoria's heart hammered in her chest, her pulse going wild. This was it. But she couldn't accept her fate. Not anymore. And she knew this was her only chance. Jameson would expect her to meekly just follow them like a sheep to slaughter.

Her body tensed up like a coiled spring, and the moment she heard the car lock click, she grabbed the handle and leapt out of the car. She heard Jameson's scream of indignation, but didn't stop. The moment her feet landed on the asphalt, she bolted into a run, crossing to the other side of the road and into the line of trees.

She fled as fast as her legs could carry her. Her lungs burned, but she pushed on. The uneven terrain made it difficult, but this was her only chance. Sure, she could end up lost, but that was better than the alternative.

It was hard to tell how long she'd been running through the forest. It could have been hours, but eventually she saw something up ahead—light. A ranger station perhaps? Damon told her they had them all over the mountain.

"There she is!" someone behind her said.

*No!* They tracked her down. Counting the two guards, and assuming both SUVs were at capacity, there were probably a dozen guys after her. Jameson had been prepared to take her at any cost, it seemed.

*Just keep going,* she told herself. If she could reach that station, maybe—"Ow!" She let out a yelp as pain shot up her leg. Her foot had tripped on a rock or a root and twisted, sending her crashing to the ground. Tears sprang to her eyes and the light she had seen up ahead blurred in her vision.

"There!" she heard a male voice say. "There she is."

Her lips clamped shut, and she tried to curl herself into a ball, but it was too late. Footsteps thundered around her, then she was hauled up. She cried out as her ankle throbbed in protest. "Stop! Please, I twisted my ankle."

"Serves you right, bitch!" A hand roughly pulled at her, the injured ankle dragging along, and the pain made bile rise in her throat.

"Please, please," she begged, hands reaching out for anything she could grab onto.

"Walk, bitch!"

A hand pushed at her back, and she hurtled forward. Pain

lanced through her arm when her elbows connected with the cold, hard ground. *This was it,* she thought. She was going to die, and she would never see Damon again.

"I'm freezing my ass off! Just kill her here," someone said. "Boss said to get it done."

"Hey, didn't you hear that?"

"Hear what?"

"It sounds like a—"

The goon's voice was cut off, as a deep, loud roar pierced the air.

"What the fuck was that?"

"Shh!"

The ground vibrated underneath her, and another bone-rattling growl broke through the silence.

"Holy fuck! It's a—"

Another roar came, followed by panicked shouts. Anna Victoria scrambled to turn around, but it was dark, and she could only see shadows. One very big shadow.

*A bear!* Her heart jumped, as at first, she thought it was Damon, but she knew deep inside it wasn't him. For one thing, this bear was much larger and bulkier. The humungous creature was on its hind feet, growling and bellowing, its long limbs stretching so it could swipe at the dozen or so men around it.

Adrenaline rushed through her, and she knew this was her second chance. Gritting her teeth, she ignored the pain and scrambled away from the chaos, not knowing where to go, but she knew she *had* to get away.

She was limping through the thicket of trees when she saw a bright light up ahead. She moved as fast as she could, but tripped and fell again. The pain was unbearable, and she couldn't find the strength to get up.

"Look what I found," a male voice sneered. "Got you, bitch."

She burst into tears when a hand roughly pulled her up to her feet. "My ... ankle ..." she managed to choke out. "P-please. Can't move."

The man who found her cursed and then bent down to haul her up on his shoulders in a fireman's carry. She would have pounded on his back, but her limbs were exhausted. The world turned upside down, and she fell limp, defeated.

"Got her, boss," the man who carried her shouted triumphantly as they stepped out into the road.

She cursed to herself, realizing she had come back to where she had started.

"Did you think you could get away from me, Anna Victoria?" Jameson shouted, his voice trembling with rage. "I'm going to kill you myself and enjoy every minute of it. Bring her here, Larson."

They continued to advance, but Larson stopped about halfway as a loud screech cut through the air. Lifting her head, she was temporarily blinded as bright headlights of a truck came into view.

Jameson screamed in fury. "Get her here, now!"

The lights shut off, and she saw the truck stop a few feet from them. The doors of the vehicle flew open, and she could have sworn two men jumped out, but they moved so incredibly fast, she couldn't keep track. All she saw were shadows moving and shifting, growing larger. A familiar, animalistic roar made hope spark in her chest.

"Damon!" she screamed.

The bear sped forward, growling as it locked gazes with her, eyes like green fire. Larson was now running like mad toward Jameson, but he was still too slow. Damon's animal rushed forward, getting in front them. Larson yelped in surprise and stopped as the bear roared furiously and stretched to full height, massive arms raised high.

"Better let her go or my friend'll tear you to pieces," came a warning voice.

*Gabriel!* She turned her head around to where he was standing behind them.

Larson swallowed audibly, then bent down and lay her on the ground before scrambling off in the opposition direction.

"Coward!" Jameson shrieked in fury.

The bear let out another roar, then turned, rushing toward the SUVs.

"Damon, no!" she screamed. Before she could even attempt to chase after him, she felt herself being lifted up.

"I got you," Gabriel soothed as he lifted her into his arms before he walked briskly toward the truck.

"You have to go after him," she said, distraught. "They have guns. Where are you taking me?"

"Need to get you to safety first." Gabriel said he gently laid her in the passenger seat of Damon's truck.

"Please, Gab—"

Gunshots cut her off, but before she could protest, he was gone. She reached for the switch for the headlights and gasped as they illuminated the scene ahead of her. A full-sized lion was leaping away, dashing toward the large bear approaching the SUVs.

She gasped as she heard gunshots. But the bear and the lion kept charging. She'd never felt so helpless, but what could she do except watch?

The lion pounced on one of the men, knocking him down. The bear, meanwhile, was surrounded by three men on all sides, holding handguns out, seemingly bent on keeping it away from the SUV where she suspected Edward was holed up. Damon's bear swiped at them, and one man shot him in the shoulder. The bear only recoiled back, but didn't fall. Another shot went off, and the bear went wild.

"No!" she screamed and slammed her palms on the dash. "Damon!"

Suddenly, a large, dark figure barreled out of the trees. It was another bear, a huge one. *The bear from the woods!* She recognized it by its size. It charged forward, taking down two of the men surrounding Damon.

Despite the shots firing around it, Damon's bear sprang into action, raking its claws down the man who had shot him and tossed him aside, then lumbered toward the SUV. Raising its arms, it brought down its giant paws on the roof and battered its own body against the side, making the vehicle rock back and forth.

*I have to get to him!* Swallowing every bit of fear she had, she pushed the door open and stepped out gingerly, then hobbled toward the rampaging bear.

She wasn't quite sure what to do, but then she heard loud sirens in the distance. Looking behind her, blue and red lights flashed in the darkness like a beacon.

*Blackstone P.D.!* Relief overwhelmed her, and tears sprang to her eyes, and she found the strength to ignore the pain and keep walking now that help was here.

"Damon!" she screamed, trying to get the bear's attention.

The side of the SUV had been ripped out, and the lower half of the bear's body hung outside. Edward's terrified screams mixed in with the rampaging bear's growls made for a bone-chilling symphony.

"Don't kill him! Please!" While she hated Jameson, she didn't want Damon to have to stand trial for his death. Plus, with Jameson's connections with those cartels, who knew what it would bring down on Damon and Blackstone? "Damon!"

The bear froze, then it pulled out of the SUV, his block head swinging around. Those familiar green eyes fixed on her. "P.D.'s here," she said to him. "Let them take care of Jameson."

The bear chuffed angrily, then shook its head. Slowly, it backed away.

Jameson's head peeked out of the remains of the SUV. His cruel eyes zeroed in on her, and he opened his mouth to say something undoubtedly smug, but suddenly froze.

"Blackstone P.D.! Put your hands up!" Three officers charged forward, weapons in hand.

Jameson's eyes popped out of his head. "Put *my* hands up?" he said incredulously. "These ... *animals* were the ones attacking me! Arrest them!"

The officers didn't seem to like what he said and closed around him. Anna Victoria couldn't blame them; after all, most of Blackstone P.D.'s officers and employees were shifters.

As the officers secured Jameson, she ran past them, toward Damon. His bear staggered back, and fell over with a loud thump. Horror filled her and she sprinted toward the animal, not caring about her ankle as she collapsed beside it in a heap. "Damon!" She buried her face in its furry hide, tears flowing freely now.

The bear's body began to shrink. Bones snapped, fur receded back into skin as she held him tight, inhaling the masculine scent of his skin. "Damon, don't die. Please, I never got to tell you that I love you."

"Y-you love me?"

She bolted straight up. "Damon?"

He struggled, but managed to push himself to sit up. "I—"

"You were shot," she exclaimed. Her eyes focused on the two bullet holes in his body—one on the shoulder and the other on the arm. While they looked horrific, they didn't seem to be bleeding out.

"Shifter healing," he explained. "Hurts like fucking hell, but the bullets went through at least."

"Oh!" Her arms wound around him and she hugged him

tight. When he flinched, she let him go but didn't move away. "Damon, I'm sorry about earlier. I was trying to get you away from Jameson. He threatened your life if I didn't—"

"Shh," he soothed. "It's all right. I know."

"You do?"

"I mean, I figured it out later, after Gabriel, J.D. and I realized you didn't go with him willingly. We saw the money and had P.D. call up Albuquerque for info about Jameson. They told us everything."

"You saw the money?" Blood drained from her face. "I can explain—"

"Later," he said. "But ... did you say you loved me?"

She took in a sharp breath and covered her mouth. "Is it too soon? You don't have to—"

"No. Of course not." Reaching out, he pulled her close. "I love you, too, Anna Victoria." Then he leaned down to kiss her.

The moment their lips touched, a strange but pleasant sensation flooded her body, warming every inch of her. It was hard to describe—like slowly being submerged in water and cocooned in a soft blanket at the same time. All the hairs on the back of her neck stood up, and a tightness wrapped around her. As she embraced Damon, she felt like they were one, bonded by some unknown force. It felt strong. And permanent.

Damon froze. "Did you feel that?"

"You too?" she asked, confused. "What was it?"

"I think ... I think it was the mating bond?"

"A bond? You never told me about a mating bond." Funnily, though, she didn't feel panicked. In fact, she'd never felt more calm or content in her life.

"It's not something we shifters talk about openly," he said. "And it's not the same for everyone, apparently."

"What does it mean?" she asked. "And why now?"

"I heard that it's supposed to happen when mates open

themselves up to each other, and there are no more barriers blocking them from accepting each other. And it means we're really mates now," he explained. "You're mine, Anna Victoria, and I love you." A deep rumble vibrated from his chest, and he laughed. "My bear approves. He likes you. Always has."

She chuckled. "I like him a lot, too."

"And me?" he asked. "Now that you don't think I'm dying ... do you still feel the same way?"

Cupping his face with her palms, she gazed into the depths of his jade green eyes. "I love you, Damon." She kissed him. "But, please don't get shot again."

He laughed—a deep, resonant sound that made her heart sing, then he wrapped his arms around her and pressed his lips to hers again. An emotion plucked a chord deep inside her, vibrant and rich, filling her with a calm she'd never felt before and making it seem like everything was right in the world.

And in that moment, she could honestly, confidently say, *it was*.

## Chapter 14

Anna Victoria insisted Damon get his gunshot wounds checked out by the EMTs as soon as more help arrived on scene. He wanted to indulge her, but only if she got her ankle seen to first, and they continued to argue as the hapless technician looked on.

"You're in pain," he said.

"You got shot. With a gun."

"That's traditionally what people are shot with."

"*Twice.*"

"I'm a shifter."

"So?" She crossed her arms over her chest, a determined look on her face.

He huffed, not believing he was going to lose his argument. But then again, he would lose every argument with her if it meant she would be by his side the rest of his life. "All right," he relented.

After they had deduced Anna Victoria did not go with Jameson willingly, he, J.D. and Gabriel had gone straight to the Blackstone Police Department Station. Police Chief Meacham had sent out the APB, but no one had reported seeing any black

SUVs leaving town. It was just their luck that an officer passing by the road that led to the mountains had seen the three black SUVs with New Mexico plates heading up.

Damon's instincts kicked in, and he knew that had to be Jameson and that he had an even more diabolical agenda than simply kidnapping Anna Victoria. He didn't bother waiting for Meacham to act and headed up to the mountains with Gabriel and J.D., with J.D. taking the road that led to HQ and him and Gabriel going up further toward Contessa Peak, the highest point of the mountains. When he saw that man crossing the road carrying something on his shoulders, he knew it had to be her. The Demon begged to be let out, and so he let his animal take over.

He thought he was nearly done for when those three guys cornered him. Shifters were tough, but they weren't invincible. Only adrenaline and rage kept him going, but if those men had kept pumping him full of bullets or shot him directly in the head, he would have died, and for a second, he thought for sure he would have. But then the sound of a familiar roar came, one he hadn't heard in a while. The giant grizzly had come down from his den and evened the odds.

*Krieger.*

Despite everything, despite his crippling fear of the outside world that made Damon's anxiety seem like a walk in the park, Krieger had come to the rescue.

But where was he now?

"Happy now?" he asked gruffly as he accepted the shirt and pants the EMT had handed him after the examination.

"Immensely." She smiled at him.

He hopped down from the back of the truck, then grabbed her by the waist, hauling her up. "Your turn sweetheart—nuh-uh." He shook his head. "No arguing."

Her lip stuck out as she pouted. "Fine."

He kissed the lip, and gave it a nip. "I'll see you in a bit. I gotta take care of something." Though both he and his bear were loath to leave her, he knew she was safe here. "Take care of her," he warned the EMT before he walked away.

Four more police cars arrived on the scene along with the ambulance. He saw Gabriel talking to Meacham, and they briefly locked gazes, but his friend waved him off, as if saying, "I've got this." He nodded gratefully and headed toward the line of trees where he last scented the grizzly.

He knew the cabin where Krieger lived wasn't too far from here, and though it was dark, he could follow the scent. Thankfully, it had stopped snowing, and he could find traces of the grizzly's scent where it brushed against the trees or broke branches and trampled shrubs. Finally, he saw the familiar cabin up ahead, the single light on the porch like a beacon guiding him. The door was ajar, so he let himself in.

"Krieger?" he called into the empty cabin. "John?"

The door to the bathroom opened and a man emerged, his frame so large, he had to bend his head to fit through the doorway. John Krieger stepped forward, body freezing as their eyes locked. "Sir," he said in his usual gruff voice.

"At ease, Sarge," he said on instinct, then quickly, "It's just Cooper now. Or Chief, if you prefer."

"Chief." He nodded.

"Thanks for the save back there," Damon said.

Krieger grunted and lumbered over to the chair in the corner, completely unfazed that he was naked. His hair had grown much longer and hung in wet strings down his massive shoulders and back, his beard left to grow into a scraggly mess.

"You missed a spot," Damon said, nodding at a smear of blood on his neck.

Krieger wiped it off with one hand. "There were more of

them," he began, as he cleaned his hand on a towel hanging from the chair.

"More of them?"

"Heard screams." He pivoted and walked to the dresser in the corner, pulling out a drawer to grab a shirt. "Went out and saw these guys chasing after that girl. Scared them off. But some of them didn't get away."

"I'll take care of them. And I'll talk to P.D.," he said. "You were protecting an innocent."

Krieger grunted, but continued to dress.

"Krieg—John." Damon cleared his throat, unsure what to say. "Thank you for saving me. And my mate."

Krieger tensed for a microsecond, then slipped his pants on. "All in a day's work then."

When Damon came back to Blackstone after his discharge, he tracked down Krieger. The man had been an even bigger mess than he was, so Damon decided to bring him to Blackstone. Somehow, he convinced Krieger to take the ranger test and do the training with him. After that, then-Chief Simpson agreed to give Krieger the permanent position guarding the entrance to Contessa Peak; after all, most shifters were social, so no one wanted this particular duty. But for Krieger, being away from everything was salvation.

Damon had visited him often in the beginning, but the guilt of what happened in Kargan had eaten away at him each time he saw the former soldier. The man's need for solitude reminded him that *he* was responsible for sending Krieger and his team into that market building, and led to the horror he endured.

"I'm sorry, John." He didn't know what else to say, but he knew he owed the other man his apology and much more. "If I haven't said it before, I'm so sorry."

He let out a chuff. "It was war, Sir—Chief," he said. "We all knew what we signed up for. No need for apologies."

"Not just that," he said. "I'm sorry I haven't been around to see you over the last couple of years. I should have visited more. I have no excuse. What you and I went through—no one else could ever understand."

Krieger turned his massive body away from him. "I don't want to talk about it," he said, his tone laced with a dangerous edge.

"We don't have to," he said. "We can just talk." He took a deep breath. "You know, forgiveness, it's not just something another person has to ask for. Sometimes ... sometimes we have to ask forgiveness of ourselves." That had been what Anna Victoria had said that morning when they were sitting outside. His throat closed up at the revelation. After all these years, it finally clicked in his brain. He'd spent all this time torturing himself, hurting himself and his animal in the process. The guilt had been eating them up alive, turning them dark from the inside. "Anyway ... I'll be by next week."

"I ... I'd like that," Krieger said, not turning around.

Damon blinked, but nodded and then headed out the door. The cool air cleared his head of the memories brought up seeing his former master sergeant, and by the time he returned back to the main road, he felt lighter. No, he wasn't completely free of guilt, but now he knew what he had to do to fix himself and his animal. However, for now, all he wanted was to be with his mate. So, he tracked her back to where she was still sitting in the back of the ambulance, a blanket wrapped around her.

"Damon!" she called as he rushed toward her. "Where'd you—oh!"

He couldn't help himself as he pulled her into a fierce hug. "I missed you."

She chuckled. "You were gone like twenty minutes." Her body sank into his. "I missed you too. Where did you go?"

"I'll tell you more later," he said. And he would tell her everything, and this could be the start of his journey to forgiving himself. The bond felt stronger now, like it was a physical thing between them, and he wondered if maybe it was because of this that he finally realized what it was his soul needed to heal. "You good to go?"

"Yup," she nodded. "Ankle's definitely sprained, but I can go home as long as I keep it iced and elevated, plus go for a follow-up with a doctor tomorrow."

"Good." Gently, he hauled her up and carried her, bridal style.

"Damon!" she giggled. "Where are we going?"

"Home," he said, looking down at her pansy-blue eyes. "I need time alone with you, mate."

"Hmm ..." She traced a finger on his chest. "Sounds heavenly."

"You're heavenly," he said. "And mine. All mine." The Demon rumbled in agreement.

Her hands cradled his face gently, and she smiled up at him, lighting up all the dark places in his soul. "Take me home, Chief."

## Epilogue

"You look beautiful," J.D. gasped as Anna Victoria stepped from behind the screen.

"Thanks—are you crying, J.D.?" she asked.

"No!" J.D. denied, rubbing her eyes with the back of her hand. "It's dusty in here."

"Sure," she teased. "Well? What do you think?" She twirled around, sending wispy light fabric fluttering around her. "Not too much?"

"It's perfect," J.D. said. "Damon's gonna love it."

In all honesty, Anna Victoria never thought she'd wear a wedding gown ever again, much less plan a wedding. But here she was, two weeks away from the wedding date. The church and caterers were booked, guests invited, tux rented, and the only thing left on her to-do list was the gown.

"This is amazing, Dutchy," she said to the redhead, who was standing off to the side. "Thank you so much."

"You're welcome," Dutchy replied. "I told you I'd have something done for you that you'd like."

Anna Victoria didn't want a gown that was too over the top,

like her last disaster of a gown had been, but she couldn't find anything online or at The Foxy Bridal Boutique on Main Street. So, J.D. suggested she turn to Dutchy for help, since the fox shifter was a fashion designer and had even made many of the gowns for Blackstone's elites.

It didn't seem like the gown she wanted existed—she wanted something that wasn't too bridal, but didn't want to stray too much from tradition. So instead of white, Dutchy had suggested a peach and blush gown, which would fit a spring wedding theme, she sketched out a design—V-neck top with a tiered tulle skirt so she could move around easily.

And now, two weeks later, she was actually wearing it. "You're a miracle worker, Dutchy. It's so much better than I thought it would be."

"See, what did I tell you?" J.D. said. "You're the best, Dutch."

"I'm glad you like it," Dutchy replied with a weak smile.

"You okay, Dutch?" The mechanic asked out of the blue.

"Me?" She shrugged. "Yeah. Why?"

"Nothing ... you seem tired."

Anna Victoria couldn't help but notice it too. Dutchy's skin seemed pale and sallow, plus it looked like she had lost weight. "You missed yoga twice in a row. You eating okay, Dutch?"

"Just stressed with work," she snapped, then covered her mouth with her hands. "I'm sorry, ladies. Really. It's been a busy couple of days." She sighed, then popped the end of her pen between her teeth. "I'll make more alterations and deliver this to you in a week. Does that work?"

"It does, thank you. Shall I see you for yoga next week?"

Dutchy chewed on her pen harder. "I'll see. I'm so sorry, Anna Victoria. I know you're trying to get your business started ... I promise I'll drop by for a class sometime, okay?"

"Of course. Whenever you're ready." Anna Victoria's roster of students and class offerings had grown over the last three months that she felt confident enough to start her own studio. She already had an appointment at the bank for a loan as soon as she got back from her honeymoon, and Catherine Lennox had even offered to become a partner and possibly put her own business degree to use by helping her manage the place.

After getting dressed, she and J.D. bid Dutchy goodbye and headed back to town. Dutchy worked out of her house, which was in a quiet little neighborhood on the west side of Blackstone.

"Are we finally done?" J.D. whined as they got into her truck. "I'm starving!"

"You're always starving." Anna Victoria rolled her eyes. "If I ate like you or Damon or Gabriel, you'd have to roll me around in a cart."

"Shifter metabolism," J.D. said proudly.

"I don't even know where you put it." She gestured to J.D.'s svelte figure. "In human *or* your animal form."

"We do *not* talk about that," J.D. said glumly. "I only told you what I was because I wanted you to pick me as maid of honor."

"As if I would ever pick anyone else," she retorted. "If anything, Damon and I were competing for you. He was hell-bent on having you as his best woman."

"If I had known that maid of honor duties included all these boring errands, I would have gone to his side."

"Well, I'm glad I won."

J.D. started the engine. "So, Rosie's?"

Anna Victoria laughed. "Of course." While she knew J.D. wasn't into the girly wedding stuff, she was glad that she agreed to be her maid of honor. J.D. had become her best friend too.

Truly, she felt honored that the other woman trusted her enough to show her, her animal. It had been a surprise, to say the least, but she promised J.D. to never tell a soul.

As they made their way to Main Street, Anna Victoria could hardly believe winter was truly behind them. Though she missed sitting on the porch watching the white stuff come down and cover everything, everything was turning green. Spring felt like a new beginning—which was especially apt because she had put the ugliness of her past behind her.

After that night Jameson had come to Blackstone, he was quickly extradited back to New Mexico, where he stood trial for the murder of Police Chief Ryan, among other crimes. Anna Victoria had gone back for the trials, and her testimony had been one of the things that finally convinced a jury to put him away for life. During her trips back, she saw her father only once. He had been cold and angry at her, probably because he was still broke, and his businesses had gone under. Though she had cried about how he had treated her, she knew that part of her life was essentially dead. Damon had soothed her, and told her everything was going to be all right.

And it was. When the ugliness of the trial was done, he took her on a trip to Hawaii, where he proposed. She, of course, said yes.

So now, here she was, planning her wedding. Neither of them wanted to wait too long, so they decided to have the ceremony as soon as they could book the church, reception hall, and get all the dresses and tuxes ready. Frankly, she'd have married him in the courthouse, but Damon's parents, his mother especially, were looking forward to having a wedding, so she didn't want to disappoint them. Carrie and Robert Cooper had come to visit twice already since they became mated, and Anna Victoria quickly grew to love them, too, and they accepted her wholeheartedly.

Finally, they reached Main Street and pulled up to the parking lot behind their destination. When they got there, Gabriel and Damon were already seated at a booth, so they joined them.

"Move," J.D. demanded at Gabriel. "I want to be next to the window."

Gabriel grumbled but got up anyway, letting J.D. into the inner side.

"Everything go okay?" Damon asked as he made room for her on his side of the booth.

As she cuddled up to kiss him on the cheek, that familiar warmth enveloped her. It was strange, but comforting. There was no way to describe the feeling she had when she was around him. From the warmth in his eyes as their gazes locked, she knew he felt it too.

"Yeah," she said. "We're all set. The catering manager at the hotel just wanted to go over a few things with me."

"Hey, ladies," Rosie greeted as she came over. "Do you know what you want?"

"I hope you didn't finish all of the special pies, Russel," J.D. nodded at the empty plates in front of Gabriel.

"They might have one or two left," Gabriel said. "Rosie, my love, I gotta tell you, that cantaloupe pie was amazing."

Rosie chuckled. "Are there any of the new pies you don't like? You're here a couple times a week now. People might start talking," she joked.

"There's just something about them ..." Gabriel looked in a daze as he stared at the plate. "They all smell so good and taste heavenly. Like I've never known what food was like before."

"Well, I'll be sure to tell my girl you like her food."

"Girl?" His head swung over toward the kitchen. "So, your employee ... is she still here?"

"Temperance?" she asked. "Maybe. She doesn't usually

leave until one but—oh, 'scuse me, kiddos." She nodded at the new arrivals waiting by the door. "I'll get your order in as soon as I seat them."

As soon as Rosie turned and walked away, Gabriel slid out of the booth and began to make his way to the pie display counter, seemingly unaware he was bumping into people. But he kept right on, rushing past the display and pushed the kitchen door open so hard, the crashing sound reverberated across the room.

"Dammit Gabriel," Damon started to rise, but J.D. waved him down.

"I'll take care of that blockhead," she said. "You guys sit tight." With a sigh, J.D. marched toward the kitchen.

"Everything all right with Gabriel?" she asked Damon.

"Who knows?" he shrugged, then flinched when he heard a crash coming from the kitchen. "I should—"

"J.D. said she'll take care of it." She slipped her hand into his. "Tell me how you are. And how Krieger is doing."

"He's ... he's doing well." Damon had told her all about his former master sergeant, and she encouraged him to spend time with him. She never asked what they talked about, and Damon wouldn't say. But, deep in her heart, she knew this was something he needed, and the best thing she could do was be there for him.

"Good," she said. "I tried on my wedding gown today."

"Oh?" He raised a brow at her. "Should we give it a test run?"

"Test run?"

"I'm sure Tim has a bottle of tequila with your name on it—ow!"

She hit him playfully on the shoulder. "Beast. You're never going to let me forget about that night, are you?"

"First of all, I'm *your* beast." The rumble from his chest—

from The Demon—sounded like one of agreement. "And secondly, of course I'm not going to forget it. That was the night that changed my life, when you walked in there and into my life."

Warmth spread across her chest and all over her body. "I love you, Damon."

"And I love you." He leaned down to kiss her, but stopped when an indignant shout came from the kitchen. "Damn, Russel," he growled. "I should—"

She took his hand as she eased out of the booth. "Let's both check on him." After all, Gabriel was now her other best friend too. "Together," she said.

"Together," he murmured and kissed her palm.

Anna Victoria enjoyed this moment, as she knew chaos was going to follow, because this was Blackstone, after all.

And she wouldn't have it any other way.

———

If you want to read a hot, sexy bonus scene from this book including that proposal in Hawaii, just join my newsletter here

http://aliciamontgomeryauthor.com/mailing-list/

You'll get access to ALL the bonus materials from all my books and my **FREE** novella **The Last Blackstone Dragon.**

Up next is Gabriel's Story!

Want to know what's in store for him?

And who is this mysterious pie maker?

Find out by reading **Blackstone Ranger Charmer**

Available at selected online bookstores.

## Preview: Blackstone Ranger Charmer

Gabriel Russel woke up that early spring morning with an urge. Urge to do what exactly ... he wasn't sure. All he knew was that he was terribly hungry, and there was only one thing that could satisfy him.

His inner lion, usually the one to protest when he wanted to get up from bed, nosed at him in an attempt to hurry him up. Somehow it knew where they were headed, and seemed to want to get there sooner than later.

"So chipper today, huh, buddy?" he told the lion. It only chuffed at him. "All right, all right."

Not many shifters talked out loud to their animals, but he and his lion had always been tight. Maybe because growing up, he'd felt lonely and it was always there for him. Most people might have thought he was crazy—after all, growing up in a household with five siblings meant he was never alone. However, there was a loneliness that came with being the youngest *and* the only male in the family that few people would understand.

Springing up from bed, he headed straight to the bathroom

to get ready for work. Contrary to popular belief, it didn't take hours for him to do his hair. Perhaps it was magic or just plain luck that his shoulder-length dark blond hair was easy to manage and seemed to come out looking perfect when he got out of bed in the morning. Of course if anyone asked his sister, Giselle, she would say it was because she had ingrained in him the importance of good hair care products. In any case, on days he worked, he usually kept his hair tied back as the first time he went on patrol, he ended up with sticks, dirt, and leaves in his hair, which neither he nor his lion appreciated.

Work didn't start until nine-thirty, so that meant he had time for a bite of breakfast before he had to make the nearly one hour drive up the mountains to the Blackstone Rangers Headquarters. So after getting dressed in his khaki uniform, he grabbed his hat and headed down to the garage. Though most of his fellow rangers lived up or nearer to the Blackstone Mountains for convenience, he simply preferred his modern loft in South Blackstone. From there, he was near almost everything in town, plus he liked the collection of shops, cafes, and restaurants that had been popping around the growing area.

It only took him fifteen minutes to get to his destination— Main Street and in particular, Rosie's Bakery and Cafe. As always, the smell of fresh pastries hit him with a nostalgic note. This was one of the places he'd go to with his father when back when he was still alive. Howard Russel would bring him here and they would sit together in a booth, just the two of them, away from the chaos of the house. Those were memories with his dad would be ones he would treasure forever.

In the last few weeks, however, coming in here gave him a different feeling. He couldn't quite put his finger on it, but it was as if he needed to be here, like this morning. After his father had passed, Gabriel would come Rosie's maybe every other month or so, and on Howard's birthday.

But now he was here three or four times a week. Not that it was a problem burning all those calories; he was a shifter, after all, and his job involved a lot of physical activity. Rosie had given him strange looks, but didn't question him on why he was here so often. Honestly, even if she did ask, he wasn't sure he could tell her because he didn't know himself why he —and his lion—was so drawn here. He only knew that he had to be here, not to mention, those new pies Rosie had been serving were irresistible. Just thinking of them made his mouth water.

"Good morning, Gabriel," Rosie, the owner of the cafe, greeted. As usual, the seemingly ageless fox shifter was dressed in a vintage dress, her vibrant red hair in pin curls.

"Good morning, Rosie my love," he replied. Most people thought he was a shameless flirt, but he'd known Rosie since he was a kid, so there was no malice there, just deep affection for the older woman who had been serving Blackstone's best pies for nearly three decades.

"First one here, as always." Rosie gestured to the dining room. "Go ahead and sit anywhere. I'll grab the coffee and you can tell me what you want."

Whistling as he walked over to his favorite booth, he sat down and glanced at the large display of pies near the back. Rosie's had a huge glass counter that features over a dozen pies everyday. Now ever since he was a kid, he had a standard order —a slice of cherry, a slice of pecan, and a slice of lemon merengue, extra whipped cream. However, recently, he'd been adventurous with his choices.

As Rosie approached, coffee pot in one hand, he opened his mouth, but the older woman beat him to it.

"Our special flavors of the day are frozen pink lemonade, toasted coconut macadamia, and Andouille Gruyere breakfast pie," she rattled off. "I assume you want one of each?"

"Thank you Rosie," he said. "And maybe a slice of cherry, for old time's sake." It had been Dad's favorite, after all.

Rosie laughed. "All right, kiddo. Be with you in two shakes of a fox tail." After filling the empty mug on the table, she sashayed back to the kitchen.

Gabriel drummed his fingers, anticipation thrumming in his veins. For nearly all his life he had that same order, until those new pies started popping up. Sure, Rosie would try a new recipe every now and then or there would be stuff that went in and out of season, but mostly the place served the basics—apple, cherry, blueberry, key lime, chicken pot pie and the like.

But ever since these new flavors came he couldn't get enough of them. It was like a taste of heaven—the flavors bursting on his tongue was like the music of angels. They were better than anything he'd have before and he couldn't get enough. The specials changed frequently, but even if the flavors were repeated, he would still order them. Those pies had almost become an obsession—the one day he came late after a shift and they ran out, he nearly threw a fit. It was like he was jealous someone else was enjoying those treats instead of him.

"Here you go, kiddo." She put four plates in front of him. "One pink lemonade, toasted coconut, breakfast, and cherry with extra whipped cream."

"You're the best, Rosie," he said, greedily eying the food in front of him. His inner lion too, licked its lips.

"Looks like you need some privacy here, so I'll leave you alone now," she said with a chuckle, then waved as she sashayed back to toward the display counter.

Gabriel reached for his fork and dug into the breakfast pie first. His eyes rolled back into his head. *God, where have you been all my life?* The pastry was flaky and buttery and melted right in his mouth while the sausage, herbs, and cheese blended together in perfect harmony. His lion too, was rolling around in ecstasy.

He took a bite of the two other pies and they were just as amazing, if not better. The cherry pie too, was great, and though he hadn't had it in a while, he could swear it was ever better than before. He had a numerous memories of sitting here with Howard after he picked Gabriel up from school, talking about his classes and friends or nothing at all. He felt keenly felt the loss of his father, but even more than that, being here brought back all the good things he'd remembered about his father before his life had been tragically taken in that plane crash along with his mother.

He swallowed the pastry and took a gulp of the coffee, washing it down. His lion was clawing at him, as if it wanted him to do ... something. Like it had this itch it couldn't scratch.

*Can't this wait, bud?* He was only halfway done with his meal.

It shook its head. *Now,* it seemed to say, its nostrils flaring.

But what did it want?

Putting the fork down, he glanced around. There was only one other table occupied and Rosie was in front of the counter, wiping down the display case as another employee was taking out the apple pie to serve it up. Behind the counter was the door that led to the kitchen. As his gaze focused on the small round window in the door, he could have sworn he saw movement behind the glass.

The lion's head perked up.

*What?*

It pointed its nose toward the door.

*There?*

It nodded, shaggy mane shaking furiously.

Gabriel knew he shouldn't ... but he was already on his feet and striding toward the kitchen door.

"Sir?" someone said behind him. "Sir, you can't go back there."

His heart hammered wildly in his chest as he placed his hand on the door.

"What the—Gabriel Russel, get away from there—"

But he couldn't hear anything except the roar of blood in his ears as he pushed the door open and stepped inside to see—

*Nothing.*

The kitchen was empty.

*What the hell is wrong with you?*

His lion protested with a yowl, then lifted its head to sniff the air. It smelled like butter, flour, pastry and sugar, plus something else in the air he couldn't quite name. Something sweet and seductively exotic.

"Gabriel?" Rosie dashed into the kitchen, hands on her hips. "What in the world are you doing in here?"

"Huh?" What *did* he do? "Er, sorry Rosie." He scratched at his head. "Didn't, er, sleep much last night. I'm still a zombie and the caffeine hasn't quite kicked in."

Rosie looped an arm through his. "How about I refill your mug, then?"

"Uh, yeah, sure." As the fox shifter gently led him out of the kitchen, he glanced back at the door as it swung close. A strange feeling came over him, like an emptiness that he never realized was inside him. *Huh.*

Shaking his head, he allowed Rosie to bring him all the way back to his booth. "Thanks, Rosie my love," he said.

"I'll get you that coffee, kiddo. It'll fix up whatever's ailin' you."

His lion once again protested.

With a last glance back at the kitchen door, he couldn't help but feel like there would be nothing that could help fill this void that somehow buried itself in his chest.

———

Gabriel didn't go back to Rosie's again since that day he barged into the kitchen. His lion didn't like that very much, but with winter behind them and spring in full bloom, he was just too busy. As a Blackstone Ranger, his work involved protecting the mountains and the forests in the area, but also since it was a park, the people and shifters who came to visit. With the snow melting on the more popular paths, the mountains were busy which meant every one of the rangers had to be on alert for hikers or campers in distress, or even shifters who may have gotten too overconfident in their abilities and needed rescuing.

But aside from that, being deep in the forests meant he could avoid—or ignore—calls from certain people and blame it on the lack of reception. Even now, as he drove to Main Street after working overtime, his phone started ringing the moment it pinged the cell towers.

Glancing at the screen, he saw the caller ID flash his oldest sister's name and blew out a breath. Genevieve was the last person he wanted to talk to right now; he knew what she wanted, but he was too tired to deal with her.

When the call went to voicemail, he let out a relived sigh, which was short-lived because his DMs now started blowing up. Checking the name of the sender, he groaned audibly. *Vicky Woolworth.* He'd rather talk to Gen and get a root canal and an appendectomy all at the same time than deal with Vicky. She was, as they said, twenty pounds of crazy in a five pound bag. While he'd broken up with her years ago, she'd pop up every now and then. He had to keep blocking her and change his number whenever she got a new number or account, but that didn't seem to stop her from trying. *Oh well, looks like I have to call my cell company again.*

As he stopped at the light, he turned his phone off, glad for the silence. Today was supposed to be his day off, but he got stuck working overtime after helping search for a lost panther cub who had wandered away from its mother. His plan had been to sleep in and meet J.D. and Anna Victoria at Rosie's after they did wedding stuff. Instead he had to shower at work and drive straight to Rosie's. When he got there, Damon was already seated at one of the booths.

"Hey, Chief," he greeted as he slid into the seat across from Damon. "Girls aren't here yet?"

Damon Cooper, who was his best friend and boss, shook his head. "Probably running late. Rogers filled me in about last night. Good job finding that panther cub."

"Yeah, she was pretty rattled, but once we got her back to her mama, everything was fine."

"I appreciate you guys staying and getting it all handled," he said.

"Of course, man. You know you can trust us for stuff like that." He patted Damon on the shoulder. "You're gonna be a married man soon, can't leave the Mrs. waiting."

At the mention of marriage and the Mrs., Damon's face lit up. "Jeeze, I can't believe it's really happening."

Gabriel chuckled. "It definitely is." And he was glad for his best friend. If anyone deserved happiness with a mate, it was Damon, especially after all the shit he'd gone through. When he returned after being discharged from the Special Forces, Damon had been a shell of what he once was. Therapy and time had helped, but he had been driving himself into the ground with work and keeping all those feelings locked up. When he met his mate, things had changed —and for the better. "So, speaking of which—your bachelor party."

Damon groaned. "No. I don't want one."

"As, c'mon man!" Gabriel pleaded. "You only get married

once, which means I only get to be our best man once. Besides, this is your last night of—"

Damon shook his head. "You don't understand. I don't need a 'last night of freedom' because as far as I'm concerned, the day I met Anna Victoria, she became mine and me, hers. Besides, my bear would never allow me to even look at another woman."

Gabriel didn't quite understand the concept of mates—no one really did. It was just one of those things shifters talked about, but couldn't explain. Most shifters didn't even meet their mates. His own parents' marriage weren't mates. But apparently, from what he'd heard over the years, mating meant a special bond tied you to another person for the rest of your life.

Frankly, it sounded like a bad deal—after all, Gabriel pretty much already knew what was in store for *his* future. That's why he was determined to enjoy his life now, while he was still free.

Lately, however, seeing how happy Damon was, he couldn't help but wonder how it would feel to have another person who was the other half of your soul.

*Ridiculous*, he thought with a mental shake of his head.

His lion, however, mewled in disagreement.

"Morning kiddos," Rosie greeted as she walked over to them, coffee pot in hand as usual. "What can I get ya?"

"Just the coffee," he said with a nod as Rosie filled the empty mug in front of him.

"And the specials for you?" Rosie asked Gabriel. "We have chocolate almond, cantaloupe, and bacon with egg."

"You got it," he said.

He and Damon chatted while waiting, but as soon as Rosie came back with their food, it was like his friend wasn't even there. He stopped listening to Damon drone on about butterfly populations or some shit, and concentrated on the delicious-smelling feast in front of him. *What was it about these pies?* He often wondered if Rosie put some kind of drug in them to make them addictive, though only he and his lion seemed to be unable to resist.

He quickly ate all the pies, with Damon rolling his eyes as he demolished them. His lion licked its lips, wanting more.

"They're here," Damon announced out of the blue.

Looking toward the door, he saw Anna Victoria and J.D., his other best friend, walk into the restaurant. As they always did, Damon and Anna Victoria instantly locked eyes and it was like no one else existed in that moment.

A strange rush of envy passed through Gabriel. His lion too, felt it and let out a whine. *Stop being a such a pussy,* he told his animal. It had been doing that lately, whenever he was around the two.

"Everything go okay?" Damon asked as he made room for Anna Victoria on his side of the booth.

"Move," J.D. groused at him. "I want to be next to the window."

With a roll of his eyes, he got up to let her into the booth.[ Alicia Montgomery 7/13/20, 1:49 PM

This is how I fixed the problem in Ranger chief :) The Ms of that was updated before release] J.D. had been one of his best friends since grade school, so he was used to her demeanor. She'd always been one of the guys—not fussy with her looks or clothes, but also fiercely loyal, which was why he liked having her as a friend. Most people thought she was dating him or Damon, and Gabriel always thought she was pretty—even if she always dressed in oversized t-shirts and baggy jeans or overalls—with her messy blonde hair and hazel eyes, but they'd known each other so long it would seem incestuous to date her now.

"Hey, ladies," Rosie greeted as she came over. "Do you know what you want?"

"I hope you didn't finish all of the special pies, Russel," J.D. nodded at the empty plates in front of him.

"They might have one or two left," he said. "Rosie my love, I gotta tell you, that cantaloupe pie was amazing."

Rosie chuckled. "Is there any of the new pies you don't like? You're here a couple times a week now. People might start talking."

"There's just something about them ..." He stared at the plates, still puzzled. "They all smell so good and taste heavenly. Like I've never known what food was like before."

"Well, I'll be sure to tell my girl you like her food."

"Girl?" His lion's ears perked up at attention. Rosie had mentioned the first time that she had a new employee or something making these pies. Why hadn't he ever asked before? He swung his head back at the kitchen door. "So your employee ... is she still here?" he asked as his heart began to thud in his chest.

"Temperance?" Rosie's auburn brows knitted together. "Maybe. She doesn't usually leave until one or two but—oh, 'scuse me, kiddos." She nodded at the new arrivals waiting by the door. "I'll get your order in as soon as I seat them."

*Go. Now.*

As if in a trance, he got to his feet, pivoting toward the kitchen. His lion roared, pushing to him move faster, until he crashed through the kitchen door.

There was someone shouting behind him, but he couldn't hear the words. He stood there, unable to move as his gaze fixed on ... *her.*

The woman was bent over the large table, dark brows knitted in concentration as she pushed out dough on the surface with a rolling pin. He could only see part of her face as she was facing sideways. However, she must have just realized he was staring at her as she lifted her head toward him.

As their gazes met, a strong feeling smashed into him. It felt like being struck by lightning, burning the edges of his nerves.

*Mine.*

And at that moment, his world turned upside-down.

**Blackstone Ranger Charmer** is available at select online bookstores. Order it now!

Printed in the USA
CPSIA information can be obtained
at www.ICGtesting.com
LVHW042247260823
756249LV00003B/355

9 781952 333118